"But I like irresponsible women, Colly."

"James, I can't let you kiss me like that again. I lose control." Colly urged him into his coat. "If we don't stop, we're going to get ourselves in trouble."

He didn't like it, but he had to agree. "You're a very sensible lady. So we should cool it?"

"Yes," Colly said, reaching for the doorknob.

"Are you really going to send me out into the freezing night?" James asked plaintively.

"I really am." Colly made a show of knotting his scarf.

"At least give me a kiss to warm me up."

Colly sighed in exasperation and gave him a peck on his forehead. "There."

"Thanks a lot," James grumbled as he left.

Colly locked the door behind him. For a moment her resolve weakened and she was tempted to call him back. The thought of spending the night in his arms was enough to sabotage even a sensible lady's good intentions....

Dear Reader,

It's May...it's springtime! Flowers are in bloom, love is in the air...*and* on every page of this month's Silhouette Romance selection.

Silhouette Romance novels always reflect the magic of love in compelling stories that will make you laugh and cry and move you time and time again. This month is no exception. Our heroines find happiness with the heroes of their dreams—from the boy next door to the handsome, mysterious stranger. We guarantee their heartwarming stories of love will delight you.

May continues our WRITTEN IN THE STARS series. Each month in 1992, we're proud to present a book that focuses on the hero and his astrological sign. This month we're featuring the stubborn, protective Taurus man in the delightful *Rookie Dad* by Pepper Adams.

In the months to come watch for Silhouette Romance books by your all-time favorites such as Diana Palmer, Suzanne Carey, Annette Broadrick, Brittany Young and many, many more. The Silhouette Romance authors and editors love to hear from readers, and we'd love to hear from *you*.

Happy Springtime...and happy reading!

Valerie Susan Hayward
Senior Editor

PEPPER ADAMS

Rookie Dad

Silhouette Romance

Published by Silhouette Books New York

America's Publisher of Contemporary Romance

 SILHOUETTE BOOKS
300 E. 42nd St., New York, N.Y. 10017

ROOKIE DAD

Copyright © 1992 by Debrah Morris and Pat Shaver

LOVE AND THE TAURUS MAN
Copyright © 1992 by Harlequin Enterprises B.V.

ISBN: 0-373-08862-0

First Silhouette Books printing May 1992

Printed in the U.S.A.

PEPPER ADAMS

As many readers know, Pepper Adams is actually two people—the writing team of Pat Shaver and Debrah Morris. Pat is a Taurus married to a Cancer. Debrah is a Cancer married to a Taurus. Our coincidental pairings give us much-needed insight into our spouses' personalities, and into our own.

When asked to write a book for WRITTEN IN THE STARS, we eagerly accepted. Using astrological signs to create characters was nothing new. For years, we have used the principles of astrology to conceive fictional personalities, to discover the basis of their attraction and to develop their conflicts.

It has been said that the indications of an individual's sun sign are only eighty percent accurate. We think eighty percent understanding is better than none. We are not experts in the field of astrology, but genuine interest, sparked by curiosity and strengthened by research, makes us comfortable writing about astrological themes.

TAURUS

Second sign of the Zodiac
April 21 to May 20
Symbol: Bull
Planet: Venus
Element: Earth
Stone: Emerald
Color: Red
Metal: Copper
Flower: Lily of the valley
Lucky Day: Friday
Countries: Ireland, Holland
Cities: Dublin, Leipzig, Palermo

Famous Taureans

Al Pacino
Stevie Wonder
Sigmund Freud
Harry Truman

Janet Jackson
Queen Elizabeth II
Shirley MacLaine
Audrey Hepburn

★

Chapter One

"Let me get this straight." With a careful eye on the bustling afternoon traffic, James Townsend braked the ice-blue Mercedes at a red light. Thinking the hearing in his right ear had failed him, he shifted the car phone to the left. "You're suspending James Jr. from preschool and it has nothing to do with bad behavior?"

The caller made no attempt to disguise her impatient sigh. Columbine Fairchild, owner and operator of the Shady Dell Preschool, wondered what kind of father didn't know that his son hated being called James Jr.

"J.J. is a wonderful little boy." She placed special emphasis on the nickname he preferred.

James wondered if they were talking about the same child. His four-year-old son could be a real charmer at times, but those times had been few and far between lately.

In fact, they'd been almost nonexistent since his ex-wife had decided motherhood was too "emotionally depleting.'' Headed for Europe to ''discover her inner capacities,'' she'd called James from the airport. Her instructions had been brief: pick up their son at day care and keep him for an unspecified length of time. It had been over three months and Lenore had yet to find herself. He suspected the search would continue at least as long as the alimony payments.

Since that call his life had been chaos, and now he had to deal with another difficult female. ''You say he's sweet, sensitive and polite. So why are you kicking him out?'' This latest complication was another aggravation, but it was no surprise. He'd already been asked to withdraw the boy from three preschools in as many months. A fact that did not bode well for his son's academic future.

''He's a very troubled child.'' The woman made the pronouncement as if she was telling him something he didn't know. Thanks for the news flash, lady. It wasn't as if James Jr. was some kind of baby Terminator or anything. He was the opposite. A shy kid made easily distraught by things other children took in stride. He cried a lot and refused to participate in group activities.

According to former teachers, his unhappiness had a way of setting off a chain reaction and before long they had a whole room full of bawling, inconsolable children. James Jr.'s unique interpersonal skills did not endear him to child-care professionals.

James tried to be patient and sympathetic, but those things took time and he never had enough of that these days. Besides, such behavior baffled him. His last care giver said James Jr. was depressed. What did a privileged kid like him have to be depressed about? He had the best clothes and the latest toys. In an effort to overcome the boy's shyness and increase his social awareness,

James had enrolled his son in all kinds of classes. So far nothing had engaged his interest.

To James, hard work was a panacea for every ill, and he assumed the childhood equivalent would take the boy's mind off his mother's heartless abandonment. An event that in itself should have engendered as much relief as it did damage. Lenore's mothering was erratic and unpredictable at best.

"Mr. Townsend, are you still there?" Colly asked. "If I'm troubling you too much, we can end our discussion."

The distraction of traffic and his own thoughts made James impatient. "No, don't do that. What were you saying?" He wondered what made this latest teacher tick. Was she one of those sour-faced women who, never having had children of her own, made a career of telling other people what was wrong with theirs?

"What part didn't you understand?" she asked.

"If James Jr. has been the darling you describe, what exactly has put you in such a snit, Ms. Fairchild?" he asked impatiently.

"I'm not in a snit," she said pleasantly. Too pleasantly.

It sounded like a snit to James. Or maybe she was just naturally a grouch. James Jr. liked her but that didn't mean a thing—his favorite character on *Sesame Street* was Oscar. "Perhaps that was a poor choice of words. Why don't you pencil me in for next Friday and we can discuss this further."

Another dramatic sigh from the other end. "I've penciled you in every Friday this month. You've missed our appointment four weeks running and I told you last week that another cancellation would not be tolerated."

"I'm a busy man, Ms. Fairchild. I have a demanding business to run."

"So do I, sir." The voice was that of a boarding-school headmistress. Cool but not quite frosty. James was getting a great mental picture of this lady.

"Then you'll understand why I don't have time for the parent breakfasts, the meetings, the pep talks, and especially the volunteering that you claim are such an important part of your curriculum. When I enrolled my son in your school, I assumed I was paying for someone to take care of him, not to fill my social calendar."

"There's more to child care than naps and story time." She was definitely frosty now. "I happen to believe, and research will bear me out, that involved parents have happier children."

"I'm sure they do. But parents who don't have time to conduct their business have hungry children."

"I see. I had so hoped to help your son overcome his problems. I regret that you won't give me the chance to try."

What came after frosty? Polar? "Give me a break, Ms. Fairchild. James Jr. likes Shady Dell."

"Yes, he does," she agreed. "He's responded well these past weeks. If you spent more time with him, you'd realize that another dismissal could be very damaging."

James swerved around a potato chip delivery truck and cursed. Maybe the epithet was for the truck driver, or maybe it was for the woman on the other end of the line. First she'd wheedled his car phone number from his overprotective secretary, then she'd used it to make him feel like the worst dreg of a parent.

"I'll be sorry to see him go," she added in case he had yet to get her drift.

"Then let him stay." James glanced at his watch in frustration. He had a couple of properties to look over before his next meeting and had no intention of speeding while engaged in conversation with this irritating woman.

"You said yourself he'd done nothing wrong. Besides, we have a contract," he pointed out.

"A contract you violated when you didn't show up this afternoon. I thought you understood that all Shady Dell parents put in volunteer time. That's how I can afford to keep the tuition low enough for families of all income levels."

He winced. Had that visit to the school been scheduled for today? Keeping one hand on the steering wheel, he flipped open his calendar. "I had an important appointment."

"Yes, you did," she agreed calmly. "You were scheduled to spend some quality time with your son and the other children as per the terms of the enrollment agreement. I made that clear when your, ah, friend enrolled J.J."

Actually, Colly had bent the rules a bit when she'd accepted the child at Shady Bell. Normally, she required an interview with the parents, but the woman who presented J.J. explained that his mother was out of the country and his father was unavailable.

She'd fallen in love with the curly-haired little boy the moment she'd seen him standing teary-eyed and forlorn in the doorway. Something about the beautiful child suggested a fragility of spirit, a spirit easily wounded. She sensed that he'd been disappointed by the grown-ups in his life, and when she learned he'd been asked to withdraw from three other schools, she'd been unable to resist the challenge. So-called problem children were her special interest.

In the following weeks the senior Townsend had failed to answer Colly's requests for an interview. Appointments had been made and broken, primarily by his secretary. It didn't take long for Colly to conclude that the boy's biggest problem was his busy, wheeler-dealer father.

J.J. didn't seem to know where his mother was except that she was in another country. A grandmotherly housekeeper dropped him off at school in the morning and picked him up in the afternoon. According to him, it was Brigit who took him to birthday parties, gymnastics class, swimming lessons, piano lessons and Tae Kwon Do. His life was so overscheduled that Colly wondered if he ever had time just to be a child.

Probably not. Which explained why he was so sad and withdrawn. The more time she spent with J.J., the more Colly disliked his father. Their conversation told her that he was self-absorbed and totally undeserving of a child as sweet as little J.J.

"My, ah, friend wasn't too sure about the details," James hedged. What an understatement. Beautiful but light in the brains department, Leigh-Anne wasn't too sure which party was in the White House. He should have read the fine print on that form before he signed it, but she'd thrust it in front of him while he was preparing for an important meeting.

He'd been too busy to do much more than scribble his name at the bottom. He'd been so relieved that James Jr. had been accepted at what Leigh-Anne called the Princeton of nursery schools he hadn't given it a second thought. Also, he'd been relieved that he and his son would no longer have to depend on someone as unreliable as Leigh-Anne for guidance. He'd assumed his only obligation would be writing the monthly tuition check.

"Mr. Townsend, I no longer have time for this. If you choose not to participate in school activities as outlined in the enrollment agreement, I will have no recourse but to ask you to withdraw your son." Colly hoped her voice sounded appropriately resolute. It was all a bluff. She had no intention of making the little boy leave Shady Dell. What she hoped to do was get the reluctant attention of his father.

James groaned and thought, *Here we go again.* Why hadn't his secretary reminded him of the meeting? Or had she? He had so many demands on his time that it was hard to remember them all, but yes, Paula had mentioned it and he'd asked her to go in his place.

"Is that an ultimatum, Ms. Fairchild?"

"Yes, I believe it is." She'd given up frosty and was now maddeningly cheerful.

He didn't like the sound of that. James's executive abilities were confined to professional matters. As the owner of a successful property management firm, he spent most of his time among the movers and shakers of the Oklahoma City business world making contacts, romancing new clients and accumulating wealth he had no time to enjoy. All things domestic were beyond his comprehension.

Life had been much simpler when he'd had only himself to worry about. He'd been a fairly good absentee father, carefully scheduling weekend outings with his small son, entertaining the boy for a few hours and then returning him promptly to his mother.

James craved tranquillity, and with those arrangements, he'd maintained control. But now he was forced to rely on housekeepers, sitters, day-care workers and old girlfriends to keep his home life humming, and the tranquillity level in his life was roughly equivalent to that in an old Marx Brothers film.

"Well, Mr. Townsend?"

"I sent my secretary. She has three children of her own and is much better equipped to help you than I am." James was frustrated that he was actually making excuses to the unrelenting voice on the phone. Unwilling to deal with the traffic and Ms. Fairchild at the same time he pulled into a convenience store parking lot.

"I don't accept substitutes, even ones as personable as Mrs. Davis."

James glanced at his watch. He was late. He was also tempted to tell Ms. Holier-Than-Everybody Fairchild that he did not accept ultimatums. Then he thought of his son. According to his new housekeeper, Brigit, James Jr. enjoyed attending Shady Dell. He couldn't begin to understand why, if the rest of the personnel was anything like the dictatorial woman on the phone.

"Frankly I fail to see how my spending a few afternoons wet-nursing a bunch of strange kids will help my son."

Colly didn't care for the man's attitude, but she held on to her temper. "It will teach him that he can depend on you to be there for him. That he can trust you to do what you say you'll do. J.J. needs that very much. More so than most children his age, because of his special circumstances."

James took offense at her insinuation that he could not be depended on. "I always do what I say I'll do, Ms. Fairchild."

"Perhaps in your business dealings things are different," she suggested.

"I'm trustworthy. Ask anyone who knows me—"

"I already have. I asked J.J."

Even as he felt himself being manipulated, James had to marvel at the woman's button-punching skills. "What did he say?" It couldn't be good. James Jr. had grown distrustful since Lenore had flown the coop.

"He said you wouldn't come."

Right. James pinched the bridge of his nose where a nasty little headache was beginning to make itself felt. "When I made the appointment I fully intended to keep it. But no certified property manager worth his salt would have missed an opportunity like I had today." Landing the management of a shopping center the size of the one he'd just signed meant maximum income with a minimum output of energy.

She was not impressed. "Any parent worth his salt would have been here, come hell or high water. J.J. was very hurt."

"It couldn't be helped. I'll make it up to him."

"Will you buy him something perhaps?" she asked archly.

That was exactly what James had planned. Little James had mentioned that he'd like to have a puppy and puppies were guaranteed to make children overlook parental shortcomings. "Of course not. I'll explain what happened."

"I'm sure he'll find that comforting."

"It's obvious that you don't like me, Ms. Fairchild. But that's no reason to punish my boy by kicking him out."

"I'm not the one who's punishing him. The stipulations are clearly stated in the contract. You knew what was expected of you and you failed to deliver." Just to make sure this savvy businessman didn't mistake her meaning, she added firmly, "The contract is now null and void."

"The least you could do is give me another chance."

"I'm afraid not."

Why was he even trying? The woman was relentless. She would have made a damned good property manager. "Can't we at least talk about it?"

"I've made my position clear. There's nothing more to discuss."

"I disagree. What if I come over there right now and put in a couple of hours?" Now why had he said that? How had this woman wrangled an offer like that out of him when he'd had no intention of doing anything of the kind?

"I don't know," she said hesitantly.

James scanned his open appointment book. He had another meeting but he could probably postpone it. And lose a chance at a deal worth a quarter of a million dollars while he was at it. He must be crazy.

But he knew that it wasn't insanity talking. It was that perennial standby of parenthood—guilt. Guilt that he and Lenore had been unable to work things out between them, even for the sake of their son. Guilt that he'd taken the easy route and spent so little time with his kid because spending more would have meant additional hassles with his ex. Guilt that Lenore had all but dumped James Jr. at a preschool before taking off for parts unknown. Guilt that he'd entrusted his son to a woman capable of doing such a thing.

"I can be there in five minutes." Guilt was indeed a motivating emotion. At this point he'd agree to almost anything to keep his little boy from being rejected again.

"You were supposed to be here at one o'clock and it's almost two-thirty. I'm not sure it would do any good now."

"Give me a break, lady. I don't know what else I can do to make it up to you."

"I'm not the one you need to make up with," she reminded him.

James tried to recall why his son liked it at Shady Dell. It had something to do with a collie. Or someone named Colly. When he'd set up the TV trays in the den last night, James Jr. had informed him, somewhat reluctantly, "Colly says we're supposed to eat at the table like a fambly."

It was time for some manipulating of his own. "Will you deny me the chance to make amends? I won't miss any more appointments."

Now there was a nice piece of fiction, but Colly would let it pass. She planned to make sure he kept that promise and any others he might be induced to make. "Can I trust you to keep your word this time, Mr. Townsend?"

"You can take it to the bank, Ms. Fairchild."

"Very well," she said with feigned reluctance. "I'll see you in five minutes."

"I'll be there," he promised before breaking the connection.

"Yes!" Colly put down the phone, jumped up from her desk and punched her fist into the air in a triumphant gesture. "Now, that wasn't so hard, was it?" She adjusted the perky yellow headband that held back her long hair, and a tall stack of yellow bangles slid down her arm.

The teachers and students were celebrating yellow today, but no one else had achieved quite the monochromatic effect she had. Of course, no one else had the wardrobe she had, either. Her flamboyant style expressed her spirit and joie de vivre. Gleaned from vintage clothing shops and thrift stores, her outfits always made a fashion statement. Today's made a full fashion proclamation.

Her billowing buttercup yellow jumpsuit, yellow vinyl wedgies from the sixties and dangling papier-mâché sunflower earrings were colorful to say the least. Fortunately, her personality was quirky enough to carry off such an oddball look.

She dusted her palms together. She'd made a believer out of his father. The next step was making one out of J.J. Sweet little J.J. who was a dream of soft blond curls, wide blue eyes and dime-slot dimples.

Colly intentionally busied herself with accounting chores. She'd let her assistant, Luz, welcome Townsend and get him settled in. She was too emotional where J.J. was concerned to deal with the man at the moment. She'd sounded bluff and aloof on the phone, but she was anything but. Like other "causes" she'd been passionate about, she had strong feelings where J.J. was concerned. Being an Aquarius, she figured it went with the territory.

Half an hour later, Luz knocked once before entering the tiny office that was squished in between the laundry room and the kitchen. Luz Maldono and Colly were as different in appearance as two women could be. Luz was short, Colly tall. Luz was dark, Colly fair. Luz wore her hair in a boyish bob, Colly preferred hers curled Rapunzel-style. Luz was as cynical as Colly was hopelessly romantic. But Luz claimed Gypsies on one branch of her family tree and insisted that that drop of Romany blood enabled her to appreciate Colly's free spirit. To the world they were opposites; in their hearts they were sisters.

Luz smiled. "I don't know how you did it, girl, but Mr. Money Monger himself has arrived." Her family had immigrated from Cuba when she was twelve and there was still a touch of Havana in her voice; in the way she said "jue" for "you," "doan" for "don't." And in the sibilant way she pronounced "has."

"Yeah?"

"He's out there doing his duty. Not too happily, mind you, but I guess we can't have everything. What did you say to get him here anyway?"

Colly grinned and her sea-green eyes twinkled. "You 'doan' want to know."

"You're right. I don't."

"What's he like?" Colly inspected the goldfish in her bubblegum-machine aquarium and pretended indifference.

"He's soap-opera handsome," Luz said with a snort. "Of course. Isn't it weird how good looks and serious personality deficits often show up in the same specimen?"

Colly laughed. "It must be a recessive gene or something."

"I think it's more of an evolutionary thing to insure survival of the species."

"You're probably right."

"But you know, Townsend doesn't seem so bad," Luz said.

The woman was a born matchmaker, and Colly knew her well enough to question her motives. "Define not so bad."

"He's okay with most of the kids. See for yourself." Luz crossed to the one-way window at the front of the office and adjusted the mini-blinds. "He's not doing so hot with our friend J.J. however."

Colly stood beside Luz and surveyed the playroom. The four-year-olds were finger painting, all except J.J. He was sitting in his little chair, staring at the paper on the table in front of him.

"You'd think his own father would know him well enough not to give him more than one color of paint at a time," Colly grumped.

Luz nodded. "First, he tried the competitive approach and told him to hurry up and pick his colors before all the good ones were gone. J.J. took so long that yellow, pink and green were the only ones left."

Colly shook her head. "Poor J.J. He's a Libra. There's only one thing he dislikes more than having to make a choice and that's having to make one in a hurry."

The other children were eagerly smearing paint on their papers, but J.J. was staring at his with a mutinous blue glare. Colly wanted to intercede but first she took a moment to size up the opposition.

James Judson Townsend was just over six feet tall, and his generous body looked fit. Not working-outside-in-all-kinds-of-weather fit, but lifetime-member-of-the-best-health-club-in-town fit. His wavy, dark brown hair swept back from a high, fine forehead and his jaw, which was currently clenched in frustration, already sported a five o'clock shadow. He could have been anywhere from five to ten years older than Colly's twenty-three years.

He was indeed soap-opera handsome.

He glanced up as if looking right at her, and Colly tensed. She knew he couldn't see her through the one-way glass, but something in his golden brown eyes said he knew someone was behind the mirror. She let out the breath she'd been holding and stared back. He had such intriguing eyes. Even at this distance she could tell they were surrounded by lashes too thick to belong to a man.

Colly straightened her shoulders and headed for the door.

Luz smiled. "Where are you going in such a hurry?"

"I'm going to try and salvage the situation before it's too late."

"Colly?"

"Yeah?"

"I know you like J.J. But this time will you try to use a little objectivity? These causes of yours tend to turn into full-time jobs."

"I'm just going to help."

Luz groaned. "Yeah, that's what I'm afraid of."

When Colly approached the painting area, J.J. looked up with a relieved smile. "Colly!"

"J.J.!" The silly greeting had become a ritual between them.

"This is my dad."

"I thought it might be." She ruffled J.J.'s blond curls fondly, then offered the same hand to his father. "Hello, Mr. Townsend, I'm Colly Fairchild. We spoke on the phone."

"You're Ms. Fairchild?" James couldn't believe it. This green-eyed beauty was the grouch? She wasn't at all what he'd expected. Instead of being pinned in an obedient bun as he'd visualized, her honey gold hair curled freely to her shoulders. She wore a blindingly yellow jumpsuit that looked as if it had been designed with color-blind cannery workers in mind. Her funky yellow shoes revealed neon pink toenails. Where were the sensible oxfords and support stockings?

He clasped her outstretched hand in his. "James Jr. talks about you all the time," he exaggerated. Actually, the kid hardly talked to him at all these days, but no point telling her that.

Colly grinned. She was enjoying Townsend's reaction. People were never quite prepared for the real her. "How boring for you."

"Not at all." James returned the smile. He liked what he saw and didn't mind if it showed. There was ethereal beauty under the clunky jewelry and outlandish clothes.

His scrutiny lasted a bit too long for comfort and she drew her hand away. Stepping over to J.J. and his blank paper, she asked, "What kind of picture will you paint?"

"Don't know," he muttered.

Colly held out the jar of yellow paint. "This would be a good color for the sun, wouldn't it?"

"Yep." J.J. stuck his fingers in the jar and came out with a sizable blob, which he proceeded to smear into a large circle on the shiny paper. He drew squiggly lines all around it and sat back, satisfied. "I'm done."

"That's a fine sun. What does the sun do?" J.J. needed encouragement and Colly knew how to give it.

"It makes things grow?" he guessed.

"What a good memory you have. What kinds of things?" Colly asked, holding the green jar out to him.

"Grass." J.J. took the jar and went to work with new zeal.

James looked on in amazement. "How did you do that? I've been trying to get him to put something on that paper for the last ten minutes."

"We'll discuss that later. Luz and I will help you at first, but in time you'll learn to manage on your own."

He noticed a faraway look in her green eyes, a look that was both dreamy and determined. It was a look of serenity, rare in one so young. Late afternoon sunlight spilled through the big front windows, seemingly with the express purpose of showing off the glints of gold in her hair.

"May I speak to you alone, Ms. Fairchild?" James asked.

She nodded. "I'm going to show your father around a bit, J.J. You keep working on that masterpiece."

When they were out of earshot, he said, "I'll come to the point. It's obvious I don't belong here. I'm not comfortable around these..."

"Children," she prompted with a smile.

James nodded. "Your idea of parents helping out at the school is noble enough, but it just won't work in my case."

"It's not an idea, Mr. Townsend, it's a proven technique. I've employed it since opening Shady Dell three years ago and I can assure you, it's been quite successful."

"Okay." He backpedaled. "Maybe it's good for some parents, but I don't know how to relate to these... children."

That she could believe. The man didn't even know how to relate to his own son, much less to someone else's. "Exactly. But you'll learn. Given time and dedication."

James was about to tell her that it was his son's education she needed to worry about, not his. If she thought she was undertaking his training, she had another think coming. Before he could say anything, two little girls started squabbling over a truck in the block area. He looked at them helplessly and then at Colly.

"Let me send someone else to fulfill the contract requirements. I employ a number of trained people who are accustomed to performing unpleasant tasks."

"Excuse me." She stepped over to the arguing girls, spoke softly for a moment and the kids' killer looks

melted into smiles. They put the truck on the floor between them and started filling it with blocks.

Colly rejoined him. "Now, where were we?" She got
that look in her eyes again and then frowned. "Oh, yes,
now I remember. Do you consider the time you spend
with your son an 'unpleasant task'?"

"No. I didn't mean that." James was thirty years old.
He'd graduated summa cum laude from Northwestern
University and earned an MBA at Stanford. He was
comfortable with oil barons, real estate tycoons and
CEOs. So why did this very young woman make him feel
so inadequate?

Colly laid her hand on his arm and led him back to the
paint area. "Don't be hasty. Let your conscience decide."

He was tempted to take J.J. and leave. Then he looked
around again. Shady Dell was located in an old residen-
tial area that had been rezoned commercial. The building was a converted 1930s era cottage with tall leaded
glass windows, high ceilings and wooden floors. It had a
big, shady backyard filled with child-size equipment.

The place was a model of cleanliness and order. Entic-
ing stacks of blocks were placed where small hands could
reach them. Colorful puzzles were spread invitingly on
low tables. In the quiet corner there was an old-fashioned
clawfoot tub painted a very contemporary shade of neon
blue. It was filled with soft pillows and picture books
meant to cushion the heads and challenge the minds of
young readers.

The shelves of toys and games were neat, the table-
tops shiny. Cages and bowls of small animals prompted
budding curiosity—lizards, newts, guppies, gerbils and
a floppy-eared rabbit. A large gray cat, whom James
surmised was Bonkers, the school mascot, that James Jr.

had mentioned, dozed on a sunny windowsill next to a big pot of red geraniums. Tape-recorded strains of Vivaldi provided a tranquil musical backdrop.

He couldn't help noticing how calm the children were and how they listened expectantly for Colly's quiet voice. Funny, but she'd had the same effect on him. He'd arrived prepared to go nose to nose with the heartless woman who'd threatened to boot his kid out of school. Now that he'd met her, he still had a physical confrontation in mind, but it had nothing to do with noses, however perky hers might be.

She didn't look old enough to be running a place like this but she was doing a good job. He was impressed by the confident, independent air of the small humans around him and knew Shady Dell was a good place for J.J. Maybe here he could learn to accept life as it was. Obviously, the school gave his son security and stability that he could not provide at home. That was a fact that bothered James more than he cared to admit.

J.J. looked up as they approached and wiped his hands on his smock. On close inspection it turned out to be an oversize, expensive white shirt that James suspected had been pilfered from his own closet.

"Since we're celebrating yellow today, I'll make some big yellow flowers," J.J. informed them.

"That's a good idea," Colly told him.

James couldn't appreciate the artwork for worrying about the smock his son wore. "Is that my shirt?"

J.J. nodded and hung his head. "We had to bring an old shirt so we wouldn't get stuff on our clothes."

James wanted to lecture him about respecting the property of others, but J.J. looked so trembly he relented. It was too late to salvage the shirt anyway. Besides, a woman who "celebrated yellow" would undoubtedly find his objections petty.

"It's okay. Let me roll those sleeves up for you. And the next time you need something, ask me."

"I will," J.J. promised.

Colly patted the boy's shoulder reassuringly. "I like your painting. That tree looks just like the apple tree in the play yard. After we have our snack, you can show it to your father if you'd like."

"Nah, he prob'ly has to go back to work. Dontcha, Dad?"

James had just been thinking that very thing himself. He glanced from his watch to James Jr. and then to Colly. Her head was tipped to one side as though waiting for him to make another mistake.

So he'd miss his appointment. It was just money. A lot of money. "Actually, I was thinking of taking the rest of the day off. Would you like that, J.J.?"

Colly felt like cheering the small victory, but she maintained her composure. "And the other arrangements?"

"You win."

"I wasn't aware we were in competition, Mr. Townsend," she lied with a sly grin, knowing full well that it had been a contest of wills from the beginning. Nothing made her day like manipulating a manipulator.

"You know what I mean. The problem is, my days are pretty full. Is there any chance I could put in some of my hours after school? I can sweep floors or cut grass or dust blocks," he volunteered. Or nibble your pretty neck. The thought had come out of nowhere.

"You'd do all that?"

And then some. "If it'll help."

Colly considered his offer. He seemed sincere but it was hard to tell. James Sr. was a handsome man who wasn't above using his sex appeal to get what he wanted. Normally, parents put in their hours during the regular school day. However, she was flexible and could see no reason not to accommodate the Townsends. James and J.J. would be together, and with fewer distractions around she could get a better perspective on their relationship.

Freed from teaching duties, she could get to know James. Not because she was interested in him, she told herself. But because she wanted to help him and his son.

She'd revised her earlier opinion, which had been based solely on telephone conversations and prejudice. Now that she'd met him, she decided, like Luz, that he wasn't so bad. In fact, he might have far more potential than she'd given him credit for. But he was inexperienced at fatherhood, a condition she planned to change. She'd never been a parent herself, but one didn't have to be sick to be a doctor.

She'd graduated at twenty with a bachelor's degree in early childhood education from the University of Oklahoma. She'd also completed special course work in family counseling and that, coupled with her unconventional childhood, made her a likely candidate to insure the education of James Townsend Sr. Before she was finished with him, this rookie dad would be a pro.

She'd have to keep her goals firmly in mind. She'd also need to continually remind herself that she had no more interest in James Townsend than in any of her other pupils' fathers.

"Ms. Fairchild?" James waited for the young woman's answer but she seemed far away.

She was back in a distracted instant. "That'll be just fine. I was planning to stay tonight and put up a new bulletin board. You guys could hang out and help me."

"Can we, Dad?" The look on J.J.'s face was expectant but reserved.

"Sure. We'll go out for a quick dinner and come back." He looked to Colly, who nodded approval. "Does that sound okay to you, James?"

J.J. shrugged, unwilling to commit himself just yet. "Can Colly come, too?"

"If she wants to." It would be good to have a third person along. Since Lenore had left, he and James Jr. didn't quite know how to be alone together.

"No, thanks," she said. "This will be a special time for you and your daddy."

James saw his son's disappointment and wished he knew how to make him smile. Or maybe he did. Despite his initial attraction to Colly, he'd decided little could come of it. She was much too young, and he feared they'd have little to talk about once they'd exhausted the topic of James Jr. Not only that, but she was a bit kooky if the shoes, jewelry and clothing were anything to go by. Strictly the down-to-earth type himself, James did not understand kooky.

On the other hand, there was nothing wrong with cultivating the friendship of his son's teacher. Maybe she could give him the insight he needed. "We'd really like you to join us, Ms. Fairchild."

"Yeah, we really would," J.J. agreed.

Colly knew she should decline. She glanced up and saw Luz's watchful eye on her and wondered what her friend would make of the invitation. She'd do it for J.J.

"Just this once." She qualified her acceptance, then smiled. "I have a rule about not dating my students."

"That's okay," J.J. said thoughtfully. "I'm not old enough to date."

"And I'd appreciate it if you would call me Colly," she told James.

He grinned. "Only if you stop calling me Mr. Townsend."

J.J. pulled on their hands. "And while we're at it, Dad, would you pleeze call me J.J.?"

Chapter Two

"I chose this restaurant because it specializes in seafood. You do like seafood, don't you, son?"

"What's seafood?" J.J. asked innocently.

"Fish," James explained.

"I like fish." He looked at Colly who assured him that she did, too.

"Now we're getting somewhere." James had patiently read aloud the choices on the children's menu. Twice. The boy was no closer to making a decision than he had been when they were seated fifteen minutes ago.

"I'll take fish," J.J. said.

The waiter shifted again, his pen hovering over his pad. "Salad or coleslaw? Baked potato, fries or rice pilaf? Hush puppies or garlic bread? Would you care for anything to drink?"

Poor J.J. That was too many choices for any four-year-old. Colly took matters into her own hands.

"J.J. and I will have baked orange roughy and rice pilaf. Hush puppies. House dressing on our salads. We'll have water to drink."

"Make that three," James told the waiter, who scurried away before anyone could change his or her mind.

"I don't know if I'll like it. I never had baked oranges before," J.J. said seriously. "But I know I like rice."

James grinned. "Orange roughy is a type of fish."

"That's good, 'cause I like oranges when they're cold."

"Brigit says you like everything you eat to be cold. She has to let his food cool to room temperature before he'll eat," James explained to Colly. "Even when he was a baby, his bottle had to be just right."

J.J. looked up, his eyes wide. "Gosh, Dad, did you know me when I was a baby?"

Colly kept her expression neutral, but the question made her sad. This little boy had been pushed into the background for far too long.

The question startled James at first, but the more he thought about it, the more he realized it was legitimate. After all, he and Lenore had divorced before James Jr.— J.J.—was two.

"Yes, of course I did. I have lots of pictures, some of us together and some just of you. Someday we'll get out the albums and look at them."

"David has a fambly, he even has a baby brother."

"Who's David?" James asked.

Colly and J.J. looked at him strangely, but it was J.J. who answered. "My frien'."

"Oh, that David." It embarrassed James that he didn't even know who his son's friends were.

J.J. went on. "I told David he was lucky, 'cause he goes places with his fambly. But he says he don't think so 'cause his baby cries a lot. Did I cry a lot when I was a baby?''

"No," James said, remembering the sweet, cherubic infant his son had been. "Even in the hospital nursery when all the other babies screamed, you were very quiet. Your big blue eyes were open wide, like you were taking in the sights and getting used to the world."

"I prob'ly didn't like all that racket. When noise gets loud, it hurts my ears."

James frowned. Another intriguing revelation. "Do your ears hurt often?"

"Not since Mom went on her bacation. She yells a lot," he added for Colly's benefit.

She would have liked to hear more about Lenore and her vacation and her yelling, but there would be time for that later. "Everyone cries sometimes," she told J.J. "But especially babies because that's how they talk to us and tell us when they need something."

"What do they need?" J.J. asked with four-year-old curiosity.

"Warmth, food, cuddling. Lots of things."

"Why don't they just learn to talk? Then they could ask for it their own self."

"They do, but it takes time because they have so many things to learn."

James marveled at Colly's gentle ways. The boy had opened up more in the past couple of hours than he had in the past three months. Or maybe James was listening for a change.

The waiter brought their salads and there was a lull in the conversation as everyone ate. Colly knew she should have a discussion with James, preferably without the benefit of little ears. She needed to know what had happened to J.J.'s mother, and especially what was to become of him.

She gathered that James did not have permanent custody and that their living arrangements were temporary. Maybe when they went back to school after dinner, she could put the boy to work dusting shelves while she talked to his dad.

Which is exactly what she did. J.J. was zipping along the bookshelves wielding the big brown feather duster and James was handing seasonal cutouts to Colly who was perched atop a step ladder. The big bulletin board was the focal point of the playroom and she was careful to make sure it was appealing, eye-catching and educational at all times.

It was the first of October, and she was replacing the September autumn leaf motif with pumpkins and scarecrows and harvest moons. In a couple of weeks when it was closer to Halloween she would add black cats and little white ghosts and jack-o'-lanterns sitting on fence posts.

Colly loved doing the bulletin board each month. It was a chance to give free rein to her creativity, and changing the decorations in the playrooms helped her mark time. It also helped the children understand the seasons and the significant events associated with each one.

"Did you make these yourself?" James asked as he passed her another construction paper scarecrow.

"I do the cutting and pasting during nap time and the children help color in the features."

"Are you a native Oklahoman?" he asked. Somehow they hadn't gotten around to small talk at dinner. They were both careful to make J.J. the center of attention.

"I was born in Colorado, but my parents are from Oklahoma. They eloped the night of their high school graduation and ran off to join a commune in the Rockies."

"You're kidding."

She smiled from her perch on the ladder. "Nope. I was born a disgracefully short time later in a tree house, delivered by a vegetarian Buddhist palm reader, who just happened to be the only midwife in the area."

"A colorful beginning."

"Very. And yours?"

"Mercy Hospital, delivery room number two, kindly Dr. Schwartz presiding."

"We can't all be pioneers, I guess."

"Growing up in a commune must have been interesting."

"The members had eclectic interests and I learned a lot from them."

"For instance?" he persisted.

"Oh, how to play the dulcimer, how to bake bread and raise organic foods. I learned conservation and ecology before they became popular issues. I also learned about astrology before it was an in thing."

James looked skeptical. "Astrology? Do you believe in that stuff? What's your sign and all that?"

"I believe the positions and aspects of the stars and planets influence human affairs and terrestrial events, if that's what you mean. By the way, what is your sign?"

He smiled. "You're the astrologer, you tell me."

"That's the kind of comment a Scorpio would make, but I know that can't be it."

"I've heard Scorpios have a reputation as great lovers. Don't I strike you as the great lover type?"

She blushed. She'd been thinking exactly that all evening but had carefully managed to conceal her feelings. "I think you're a Taurus."

He looked surprised. "That's right. May tenth is my birthday. Hey, you're pretty good. You don't read minds, do you?"

"No. We moved back to Oklahoma City before I learned to do that."

He grinned so she would know that he knew she was teasing. At least he hoped she was. "Why did your parents leave the commune?"

"The revolutionary seventies gave way to the yuppie eighties and my folks had a growing family to support. They opened a stained glass studio and called it The Flower Child in honor of their former life-style."

"I've heard of it. Isn't it in the Paseo district?"

"That's right. Anyway, I got my first taste of real school at the advanced age of thirteen."

"You mean you'd been playing hooky all those years?"

"Hardly. Like the other commune kids, I was taught by a lovely man we all called Professor. He was a genuine Renaissance man and taught us all about art and language. He took us hiking and taught us botany and ecology. Fishing trips turned into biology lessons, bread baking and candle making into physics. We thought flying a homemade kite on a windy mountaintop was fun, but to Professor it was a chance to study aerodynamics. He always told us, life is the best lesson of all."

"He sounds like a fascinating man."

"Oh, he is. I still keep in touch with him. He's the only one left at the original Shady Dell."

"You named your school after your old home?"

"Professor told me it would bring good luck. He's my mentor and the real reason I went into early childhood education. Public schools do the best they can, but they fall short in many ways. I believe that if a child's creativity and self-expression are challenged early enough, he will have the strength to handle a cookie-cutter school later on."

James looked at Colly in amazement. No wonder J.J. liked it here so much. He almost wished he were four years old again and could have the benefit of such a gifted teacher. But then, he wouldn't be able to appreciate her as a woman.

"Did you have trouble adjusting to real school after the freedom of the commune?" he asked as he passed her more decorations.

"I thought it was rather humdrum. I love books, but it was strange to learn everything out of them when I was used to learning from the world. Thanks to Professor I knew enough to go into accelerated classes. I graduated from high school when I was sixteen and went straight into OU. I was only twenty when I earned my degree and I had a hard time getting financial backing for my school."

"But determined woman that you are, you persevered," he guessed.

Satisfied with the bulletin board, she climbed down from the ladder and perched on the edge of a table. The fat gray cat sidled up to her and she took him in her lap. "Nice Bonkers," she murmured, a dreamy look on her face.

James was distracted by the movement of her hand in the cat's fur and wondered what it would be like to be on the receiving end of such tender attention.

"Actually, I lucked out." She came back from whatever mental vacation she'd taken and answered as if three whole minutes had not passed since his last comment. "I found a loan officer who was desperate to find a good preschool for her children. She liked my ideas and approved the loan. Of course, my parents had to cosign because I wasn't twenty-one."

"And how old are you now?"

"Twenty-three."

"So young?"

"You make it sound like an ailment."

"No. I meant you're very wise for your years. And mature."

She laughed and made a face. "Oh, I hope not. I don't mind being wise, but I don't think I'm ready for mature." She jumped up and fetched a large green watering can from under a table. She filled it at the sink in the corner and went about watering the many plants hanging in baskets and lining the windowsills.

James didn't quite know what to make of her last comment, but now that he knew her background he understood why she was such a natural teacher. Her parents and others had obviously taught her to respect individuality. To value the qualities that made each person unique.

He watched her move around the room, pinching off a dead leaf here, turning a pot there. When she passed J.J., who was still into industrial dusting, she paused long enough to give him a smile and a reassuring pat. The look his son gave her in return nearly broke James's heart. J.J. had never given him such an open look of respect and admiration and... and what? Love? He was pretty sure Lenore hadn't received one, either.

The look said that J.J. felt special to Colly. And maybe that was her gift. She earned the trust of her young charges by making each of them feel unique.

There was that word again. Unique. It cropped up often in thoughts of Columbine Fairchild because it was such an accurate description. She was one of a kind.

"Do you want to help us feed the critters?" she asked him.

"Sure. What do they eat?" He joined Colly and J.J. beside the array of cages.

"Critter food," J.J. piped up. It was the closest thing to a joke James had ever heard his son say. Hearing that little boy's attempt at humor made the pain of losing out on a quarter-million-dollar deal less traumatic.

When all the chores were done around the school, James and J.J. took their reluctant leave. James thought if it were up to his son, he would happily and permanently move into Shady Dell, lock, stock and *Sesame Street* toothbrush.

"You men drive carefully," she told them as she locked up. The autumn night was mild and the sky was gaudy with stars.

"See ya tomorrow, Colly," J.J. said hopefully.

"Tomorrow's Saturday," she reminded him. "You didn't forget about David's birthday party, did you?"

"Oh, yeah! Dad, can I go? I know just what I want to get him for a present."

"I guess you're going then."

"Goody. It's at Show Biz Pizza. You know pizza's my favoritist food, dontcha, Dad?"

As a matter of fact, James didn't know that but he'd keep it in mind. "Good night, Colly."

"Good night, James. We'll keep in touch."

"I hope so," he replied. "You have all my numbers."

Colly waved as she climbed into the ancient Volkswagen bus that had belonged to her parents. The painted peace symbol and rainbow on the side had faded, but her memories of those happy childhood days had not.

She had his number all right, and it looked like she had her work cut out for her. She would educate James Townsend in the fine art of parenting and he would be an apt, if stubborn, pupil.

Anyone who knew anything about astrology knew that Taurus men made loving, responsible, affectionate fathers. Now that she knew him better, she realized he was not the hard-hearted, callous man she had thought him.

He obviously loved his little boy. He was just busy, successful, ambitious. And lonely. Maybe even a little bitter. She'd been unable to glean any information about his ex-wife or their relationship. His reluctance to discuss the matter indicated unresolved problems.

She'd show him the way and someday he would thank her for it. Knowing the Taurus resistance to being pushed and prodded—even in the right direction—she would have to plan her strategy carefully. Better to make the stubborn bull think any changes were his idea.

Lucky for James, she was conceited enough to think she knew what was best for everyone. Luckier still that she understood his hardheaded Taurean personality. A less arcane woman might be put off by his deliberate manner. Little did he know that Aquarians could be just as stubborn—no, make that as determined—as any Taurus ever born in the month of May.

Driving home, James tried to understand his confusion about Colly. At first she'd seemed cool toward him but she'd warmed up once she'd gotten her way. Still, he felt she was judging him somehow. What did she want from him, anyway? He'd kept their appointment, missing a very important meeting to do so. He'd put in the hours she demanded, but in truth it had been no hardship.

And yet, all evening he sensed he hadn't measured up. Not only to his son's teacher's standards, but to his son's.

"We're home," he announced to the sleepy child beside him.

Home was a sprawling condominium unit owned by his company. James had received two lucrative bids on the property just this week and that meant they'd be moving soon. He had no sentimental attachment to property and didn't own any that he wouldn't sell if the price was right. The offers he'd received had been more than right.

Having J.J. would complicate things. All that moving around would be harder to accomplish. Who would believe that such a little kid could have so much stuff? Maybe he should think about settling down in one place. Get a real house with a yard and a swing set. They could even get that puppy. The problem was, he didn't know if he should make his living arrangements with J.J. permanent. Everything was still up in the air.

Lenore had court-ordered custody and even though she'd been gone for over three months, it was possible that she would breeze back into town at any moment, sweeping J.J. out of his life and into the shadow world of weekend visitation.

At first, he'd longed for just that. When the daily distractions of domestic life got too much to handle, he'd wanted nothing more than to see his son safely in his mother's keeping. But now the thought of giving him back caused conflict. Lenore wasn't much of a mother, and he was no great shakes as a father, either, but he'd gotten used to the kid and all the complications he caused.

Maybe he could change. Colly seemed to think so. She'd told him that good fathers were made, not born.

There was also the chance that Lenore might not come back. Was he ready for that? Was he equipped to be a full-time, card-carrying single parent? Could he deal with all the little daily nitty-gritty that drove people crazy? Did he want to? The thought of being solely responsible for his child for the next sixteen or so years gave him goose bumps.

But that probably wouldn't happen. His ex-wife would never relinquish custody, not when it meant so much to. her financially. She'd be back eventually, ready to pick up where she'd left off. He was angry at Lenore for being so insensitive to J.J.'s needs. He wasn't a baby anymore. He couldn't be shuffled back and forth without emotional damage.

James parked in the garage and carried J.J. inside. He felt a tightness in his chest as the small body relaxed against him. He was getting attached to this mixed-up little person.

He knew that was a strange way to think of his relationship with his own son. People got attached to favorite chairs, loyal dogs and broken-in jeans. The word had nothing to do with love, and James did love J.J. But emotionally he'd been *detached* for most of the child's life.

He helped J.J. into his pajamas, tucked him into bed and pulled the colorful comforter up to his chin.

"Good night, Junior."

"Dad?" he asked softly.

"Yes?"

"I'll be five soon, right?"

"That's right, October eighteenth."

"I'm not a baby any more, am I?"

James wondered where this was leading. "No."

"David says Junior's a baby name. Ever'body at school calls me J.J. Can't you call me that, too?"

He smiled at his son. "I'm sorry. I forgot. Good night, J.J. Dream a little dream for me."

"'Night, Dad." That settled, he snuggled into the pillow and closed his eyes.

James went into his own room and sat down at his desk to go over a management proposal he had to present Monday morning. But his brain refused to concentrate on cost factors. All he could think about was the instability of his little boy's life.

James's own father had died when he was three. His ambitious mother had used the insurance money to go to law school. He didn't have a stay-at-home, cookie-baking, field-trip-chaperoning parent and he wasn't emotionally traumatized by the experience. Or was he? A shrink would probably say that his own lack of family life had contributed to the breakup of his marriage.

Lenore had accused him of being selfish and interested only in his business. She hadn't understood that the reason she got to buy all the things she wanted was that he worked hard for her. But had his family's security been the real reason he'd absented himself from so much of their lives?

Truth to tell, he'd been afraid of failure. He'd worried about that during the dark hours before dawn many nights. He couldn't stand being no good as a husband and father. It was better not to try too hard. He feared he might be one of those people who possessed no familial instincts.

After his divorce he'd given up all hope of ever being the kind of father he imagined other men were. But Columbine Fairchild had restored that hope. In one short evening she'd made him believe that anything was possible. On one hand he resented her interference, but on the other he was relieved. Maybe that's what he and J.J. needed—an interested third party to show them the way. If there was a way.

He soon gave up thoughts of work and went to bed. Tomorrow he'd show J.J. those photo albums if he could remember which box they were stored in. Brigit had the weekend off, so later he'd take him to the mall to buy a birthday gift for his little friend. Then it was off to David's party at the pizza place. It was an ordinary way to spend a day, but James was actually looking forward to it.

Just as he was looking forward to seeing Colly again. Even if she was just his son's teacher and not his type at all. He liked his women over twenty-five, sophisticated and less demanding than the whimsical Colly. She'd found him an unsuitable parent and probably found him an unsuitable companion, as well.

So, what did he care? Now that he thought it over, he was ashamed of himself for flirting with her the way he had. He'd been so busy lately that his social life had been unplugged. All he needed was a little female companionship. He made up his mind to call one of his old girlfriends and make a date for next weekend. Maybe he'd call Leigh-Anne.

Nah. After the stimulating conversation he'd had with Colly, an in-depth discussion about Leigh-Anne's new peel-off nail polish would be depressing. He'd call someone who could keep his mind off a certain free-spirited kook.

He now had a plan and felt better for it.

"Colly, are you listening to me?" Luz demanded as she twisted around to get a better look at the back of the wedding gown she was trying on.

"I told you I'm out of my element in these trendy mall stores. Listen to that music. It's cranked up too loud for relevant conversation."

"I don't need relevant conversation," Luz protested. "I need your opinion."

Colly winced when another rock song began. "Why not look for a gown with a history? It would be so much more interesting."

"A used wedding gown?" Luz made a face. "Ugh."

Colly sighed. Another thing they differed on. Luz liked everything new and up-to-date, and Colly liked clothes that whispered of the past when she wore them.

"What do you think of this one?"

"It's okay," Colly replied without enthusiasm.

"Come on, girl. You got a great sense of style, that's why I dragged you along."

"I don't think you really want me to pick your dress, Luz."

"If you help, I'll show you a nifty little wood shop where they make those cute old-fashioned toys you've been wanting for the school."

Colly perked up. "Here? In the mall?"

"That's right. I'll show you where it is, but first we have to find the perfect dress."

"You're not getting married for a year."

"I know that. But a girl has to plan ahead. Perfection takes time." Luz turned to face her. "Now, what's your honest opinion?"

"It's a bit fussy?" Colly guessed.

"That's what I thought, too. I'm too short for so many ruffles."

"And it's too pristine. Try the antique white one, it'll look better with your dark complexion."

"Girl, now you're cookin'. That's the kind of advice I knew I could count on from you."

After trying on a dozen more dresses, they found one Luz could not live without. Maid of honor Colly was next to be outfitted. She was hard to please because she refused to wear anything that "made her look like one of those silly dolls old ladies keep in the center of their beds." It took several trips around the store before she spotted a dress she would consent to wear—a lace sheath in an old-fashioned color called ashes of roses. She'd find her own accessories, thank you.

Luz agreed because she knew Colly's special flair would make the outfit unique. They spent another hour in the store while the alterations lady tucked and pinned, but finally they were free.

Colly was delighted by the treasures in the woodcrafter's shop and purchased several new items for the playroom. She also found a wooden dancing clown for David.

As they left the mall, the two women heard a small voice calling them. They turned and saw J.J. running toward them on sturdy legs. James was right behind him. Colly's heart pounded with excitement at the sight of the tall man approaching them. He walked with purpose as though nothing could deter him from whatever course he set for himself. Sunshine streamed through the skylight overhead and washed him with a brightness that illuminated the planes of his handsome face.

Clasping J.J.'s hand, James greeted the women and noticed the pleasure etched on Colly's features. Her eyes had widened when she spotted him, her spontaneous smile a genuine reflection of her feelings. Knowing that she was as happy to see him as he was to see her elevated an ordinary day to extraordinary status.

"I thought you only shopped the vintage clothing stores," James teased Colly with a glance at her bulging shopping bags.

She smiled and placed the blame on her friend. "Luz dragged me here."

"Kicking and screaming," Luz put in with a wink at J.J.

James noticed Colly's brocade Nehru jacket and black stirrup pants and decided that she hadn't bought them in any retro-60s boutique. Hers were the genuine items. She carried the look off with finesse, distinguishing herself from the cookie-cutter yuppie style of the other shoppers. When he found himself speculating about her lingerie wardrobe, he decided it was time to excuse himself.

They talked briefly, compared birthday presents and parted with a promise to see each other later at the party.

After the Townsends left, Luz turned to Colly with an ornery look on her face. "Did I detect a spark of electricity between you two?"

"Between me and J.J.?" Colly asked innocently.

"Come on, girl. You lust after the kid's old man, don't you?"

"Lust is hardly the word. I'm interested in them because I think they need help. I don't have any secret motives."

"Oh, sure."

"J.J. needs stability in his life and I plan to see that he gets it. Children must have someone they can depend on. That little boy is nearly five years old and there isn't a single person in whom he can place his trust."

"He trusts you."

"You know what I mean. I'm a teacher. I'm temporary. He needs someone permanent. He needs his father."

"I know all about you and your lost causes. It may come as a surprise to you that James Townsend is more interested in you as a woman than as his son's teacher."

Colly's shrug was eloquent. "If that's what it takes to get his attention, then so be it."

Luz's brown eyes opened wide. "You'd go so far as to have a relationship with a man just to get him closer to his son?"

"I told you I'm committed."

"I think you should *be* committed. If you have a yen for J.J.'s father, go for it. But if you have any sense at all you'll be honest with yourself. Otherwise, somebody's gonna get hurt, and it could be you. You're always trying to fix the world. You should know by now that some things are past repair."

"This time I can help."

"Famous last words, girl."

"He's a Taurus so I have to make James think everything is his idea. The bull wrote the book on hardheaded behavior, but he's so positive he's un-scamable that he'll never notice the scam. Don't worry, I know what I'm doing."

"So do I. You're using astrology as an excuse to manipulate James Townsend into doing what you want him to do."

"Those are harsh words, Luz."

"It takes a conniver to know a conniver."

"The stars don't compel," Colly assured her.

"They impel. I know all about that, girl. I also know all about you."

The party was a blur of mechanical singing animals, spilled soft drinks, blaring video games and pizza. In other words, it was the epoch of social achievement for a five-year-old. Colly didn't usually attend her students' parties, but David's mother was a special friend and Colly had known the boy since infancy. When she had a chance, she got James off in a reasonably quiet corner for a talk. Her horoscope had indicated that she could mix business with pleasure successfully tonight.

"I'm very concerned about J.J.," she said.

James looked around and saw his son gunning away at a bunch of exploding asteroids on the screen of a nearby video game. "Why? He seems to be having a great time."

"I'm not talking about tonight."

James sighed. "I know, I know. He daydreams a lot and doesn't pay attention," he recited, ticking off the faults other teachers had found. "He's stubborn and refuses to participate and when he's pushed he cries. I've heard it all before."

"Well, no," she said in confusion. "He's not like that at all."

It was James's turn to be confused. "He isn't?"

"J.J.'s delightful. He's bright, responsive and very creative."

This was new. He'd never heard that from any of James's other teachers. "He is?"

"That's one of the things I wanted to discuss with you. I just don't understand how it is that you know so little about your own son. Is J.J.'s mother ever coming back from her vacation?"

He frowned. "I don't think that's any of your business."

Colly sensed she'd overstepped the bounds, but she wasn't about to let that stop her. "I'm his teacher and I care about him. You can tell me anything. Is his mother terminally ill?"

"Not unless you can call immaturity and irresponsibility an illness. Why do you ask?"

"I got the impression she might be sick from J.J.," she said. "One day David asked him when his mother was coming back and he replied, and I quote, 'maybe never.' I thought illness might be the reason for her prolonged absence."

"As far as I know, Lenore is healthy."

"I'm not trying to be nosy. I think I could help J.J. deal with his circumstances better if I knew what those circumstances were."

James didn't look at Colly. He focused his attention on the singing mechanical bear. "Lenore takes off every now and then. It's just something she does. She usually comes home after a couple of weeks."

"How long has she been gone this time?"

"About three months."

Colly gasped. "Three months!"

"She's trying to find herself and when you're as mixed up as Lenore, it takes a while."

"So do you have custody of J.J.?"

"No."

"Are you going to petition the court to obtain custody?"

"I haven't thought about it." James sighed. "Look, I'm new at this. I don't know all the answers."

"What if she decides to come back?"

"Oh, she'll be back all right. She lives on alimony and child support. She hasn't had a check since she left and I expect her any day now."

Colly was appalled. "She hasn't even telephoned to check on her own son?"

"No. She's the trusting sort." James stood up, ready to put an end to the conversation. He'd hoped to have another neutral chat with Colly, maybe even ask her for a date. Instead, her probing questions had put him on the defensive.

"What sort are you?" she asked bluntly.

"I don't think I want to answer any more of your questions. Is there anything else you need to know to teach J.J.?"

"I'm sorry. It's just that I think he would be happier if he had some security. If he knew he was a permanent part of your life."

"I'm not so sure about that. My life-style isn't geared for raising children alone."

"You told me the other day that you employed a large number of people who'd been trained to handle unpleasant tasks," she reminded him.

"So?"

"So let them handle the work while you concentrate on your son." The solution seemed so simple, Colly couldn't understand why she even had to mention it.

"Are you trying to tell me how to run my life, Colly? Because if you are, you can forget it. I've been managing just fine for years."

She looked at him critically, but in such a way that he could hardly take offense at her next question. "How have you been doing the past three months?"

Chapter Three

Colly immediately realized that her last question had been a tactical error. James slumped back in his chair, crossed his arms and glared at the mechanical musicians, refusing further comment. She'd known it was fatal to push him, yet she'd been unable to stop once she'd started. Now, in true bull-like fashion, he was sitting there like a chunk of cold stone, refusing to speak another word.

"The band's pretty good," she said with a teasing grin, hoping to cajole him into a better mood.

James kept his gaze glued to the stage and shrugged. "If you like singing gorillas."

Sometimes drastic situations called for drastic measures. It was too noisy and distracting in here; she'd have to get him alone to do any good. Knowing Taurean males were gallant to a fault, she concocted a scheme.

She saw him watching her out of the corner of his eye as she slipped into her jacket but he didn't say a word.

She paid her respects to the hostess and wished the birthday boy many happy returns. When she came back to the table for her purse, she asked James, "Would you mind walking me to my van?"

He looked up curiously, but made no move to rise.

"That is, if you're not too angry with me?"

He stood up. No matter how irritated he might be by her know-it-all attitude, he wouldn't let her walk to her van alone in the dark. "I'll let J.J. know where I'm going and meet you at the door."

A few minutes later, he held the door for her and they stepped outside.

"Ah, auditory relief," Colly said, appreciating the silence of the parking lot. "The people who work in there must wear earplugs."

He made no comment and they walked side by side without speaking or touching. She fished her keys out of her purse and turned to him. "Come on, James. I'm sorry if I hurt your feelings."

"You did not hurt my feelings," he assured her.

"Then I'm sorry if I overstepped my limits."

"If?" He glanced at her briefly and it was a look full of meaning.

"Okay, I made a mistake." She was careful not to promise it wouldn't happen again. She wanted to be as honest with him as possible.

"Yeah," he mumbled.

She unlocked the van door. "I apologize," she said softly. "I'd like us to be friends."

"Is that what you want us to be? Friends?" He was a little disappointed with the way their second meeting had gone. But for some reason, he didn't think he'd feel so bad about things if he kissed her. He wondered what she would do if he did.

James's face and intentions were well lit by the tall security light. He wanted to kiss her, that much was obvious in the eye contact he maintained. It was up to her to put an end to such intentions by looking away, but she couldn't do it. She told herself she didn't want the kiss to happen, that she shouldn't let it happen. And yet she had no wish to prevent it.

At that moment, her response to him was strictly sensual, and rational thought seemed pointless. She liked the way he made her feel and her gaze remained locked with his.

James took a step toward her. Feeling confused by the messages her own body was sending her, she swallowed hard. "Are you going to kiss me?"

"Unless you have objections."

"I think you should. If you don't, the fact that we didn't kiss when we had a chance might become a bigger issue between us than the kiss itself."

"I'm not sure I follow your logic, Colly, but I'm happy to oblige you."

His lips covered hers. The kiss was tender, full of promise and meaning, and she gave herself up to it. It would be easy to become infatuated with a man who could evoke so much feeling with a kiss, she thought as she tried to excuse her inexcusable behavior. There was real intimacy in the kiss and she wasn't sure she was ready for that.

What she felt was more than a desire to help J.J., more than a need to manipulate the situation to a positive outcome, more even than an infatuation. She felt a nameless emotion when James kissed her, but she didn't have the experience necessary to deal with it. Colly knew she should end it before his effect on her became a real menace to her emotional independence.

But it was difficult to hold on to that train of thought once he parted her lips and slid the tip of his tongue into her mouth to deepen the caress. In that instant she forgot all about J.J.'s needs and concentrated on her own. She was mindless of everything except the tingling pleasure she felt.

James was elated by Colly's response and more than a little overwhelmed by his own. He was going down for the count, and every nerve ending in his body screamed for more. He yearned to be closer. He was already wrestling with the buttons on her jacket to achieve that closeness when he remembered where they were.

He struggled for control, reminding himself once more of the reasons he should stop; they were in a well-lit parking lot and someone could pass by at any moment. If they didn't stop now they could soon be totally embarrassed. Drawing on his reserves of strength, he ended the kiss but could not relinquish her from his arms.

She allowed him to hold her for a moment, then pushed herself out of his embrace. Raising her eyes to his she tried out her voice and found it rather squeaky. "I almost wish you hadn't done that."

"Why?"

"Because I wanted us to be friends."

"I was feeling darned friendly there for a while. I think you were, too."

"We have to forget it ever happened. That's what I'm going to do." Yeah, right. It was a dumb remark and she knew it.

He touched her cheek. "I'm not sure I can."

She had to think of J.J. She wouldn't be able to help him if she became emotionally involved with his father. She could have only one passion at a time. For that reason, she tilted her chin up and told him another fib. "It was just a kiss, and as kisses go, it wasn't bad."

James smiled. She would never make a good card player. "I guess I must have missed something. Maybe I was so caught up in my own feelings, I didn't notice your revulsion?"

"I didn't say I didn't like it." She couldn't say that. Cause or no cause.

"Oh?"

"You've entrusted your son's care to me."

"And?"

"I have scruples, you know."

"I know, but they didn't seem to get in our way just now."

"Okay, it was my fault. I take responsibility and I won't let it happen again."

"Is that some kind of affirmation or something?" he teased.

"Under the circumstances I think the only kind of relationship we should have is a platonic one."

"Let me see if I have this straight," James said. "You did enjoy kissing me?"

"Yes, but—"

"But you don't like me?" he finished for her.

"No, no," she said too quickly. "It isn't that. As a matter of fact I like you more than I expected to."

"Is there someone else?"

"No," she said.

"I don't see the problem."

"As your son's teacher, it wouldn't be ethical or professional for me to get involved with you."

"I can see how that could be a problem. I can always take J.J. to another school," he suggested. He didn't mean it, of course, but Colly took him seriously.

"You can't do that."

"Then what do you suggest?"

"I already suggested it. We can just be friends."

"When J.J. starts kindergarten next fall, you won't be his teacher any longer," he pointed out.

"True, but—"

"Then we only have to get through a few months of this platonic stuff before we—"

This time Colly interrupted him. "Why don't we just take it one day at a time and see how it goes?"

"That's a start," he said, reaching up to wind a golden strand of hair around his finger.

She giggled nervously. "Who knows, by the time J.J.'s graduation rolls around in the spring, you might be more than happy to see the last of me."

He studied the way the silken curl circled his finger. "I doubt that. I can be a very patient man."

"Not many men are that patient. Besides, it's several months until spring and I want you to know if you decide to try your luck elsewhere, I'll certainly understand."

"So you give me permission to see other women?" he teased.

Realizing how ridiculous that sounded, Colly flushed. "I just meant that I'd understand if you lost interest."

"I admire understanding in a woman."

"Are you making fun of me?"

"Absolutely not. I'm just not accustomed to being this honest this early in a relationship."

"It's only fair to tell you up front that I'm a bit flighty where men are concerned."

"Like a butterfly?" he questioned softly as his hand curved around her neck. "Do you bring pleasure to one man's lips only to flit away to another's?"

"I didn't say I was promiscuous," she denied flatly.

"I never for a moment meant to suggest you were," he said honestly. In fact, he suspected the engaging Ms. Fairchild had had little experience dealing with any males over the age of six.

"It's just that men and I don't seem to be on the same wavelength for very long." When Colly got nervous, as she was now, she babbled. "Luz claims I'm a slow starter. She says by the time I get to know a man well enough to... well... you know, the attraction's already worn off."

"Maybe you just haven't met the right man."

It was her turn to smile. "That's what they all say."

"I didn't mean it like that. I wasn't implying that I'm the *right* man, but I'd like a chance to find out for myself if what we feel might turn out to be bigger than both of us."

She appeared to consider and her eyes got that faraway look in them again. "Anything between us would have to be strictly platonic," she said at last. "Can you handle that?"

"I can if you can," he said, wondering if either of them could abide by her silly restrictions. "A guy can't have too many friends."

"You're willing to settle for that?" she asked, mildly disappointed that he wasn't trying a bit harder to talk her into something more.

"Absolutely," he replied, thinking all the while that friends could become lovers. He took her right hand in his and they shook on it.

James climbed onto the step stool and secured the jack-o'-lantern cutout to the bulletin board. He leaned down and selected a black cat from the assortment Colly held up to him. He'd stopped by Shady Dell many times after hours. He'd even managed to work in a parent breakfast on his way to work this morning. He found he enjoyed the time he spent with Colly and J.J. The first time, he'd thought it was Colly who made things so much fun.

But now he wasn't sure. In two weeks, J.J. had made unbelievable progress. He was becoming more open with James and no longer cried over little disappointments. He took a more active interest in the things that went on around him, and the positive changes in J.J.'s attitude were heartening.

The change in himself was the real surprise. He never got around to making a date with anyone else and didn't think he would now. He felt more content and didn't need to be wheeling and dealing all the time to feel that he had a life. Living under pressure was a habit he'd have to wean himself from slowly, but he no longer thought it would be impossible. He looked forward to spending time with J.J. and tried to pick him up from school when his schedule allowed. After only a few hours of what Colly called quality time, they no longer found it so difficult to talk to each other.

"Put that pumpkin a little higher," Colly instructed him. Her horoscope had warned that she would delight in all things sensual today, so she made an extra effort not to be too delighted by the play of muscles that went on beneath James's knit shirt as he reached to place the decoration.

Her behavior toward him had been impeccable since the parking-lot soul-searching episode. But what harm was there in noticing that he had been blessed with nice buns? Or that his thighs were incredible? The movement of said thigh muscles was almost hypnotic as he relaxed them, then stretched and relaxed again.

James glanced at J.J. and found his son's attention fully absorbed by the baby lizards he was supposed to be feeding. He lowered his voice and asked Colly, "Can we talk a minute?"

"That's what I'm here for," she said in an effort to remind herself of that fact.

He climbed down from the step stool. "I wanted to discuss J.J.'s birthday with you. He says sometimes kids have their parties at school."

Colly switched mental gears from muscles to birthdays. "It depends on the party. I'd have to approve your plans beforehand."

For a moment she'd had that familiar dreamy look on her face before she got down to business. "Don't worry, I'll take care of all the arrangements."

Colly was pleased at this new development. James was thinking of the future and taking responsibility for J.J.'s happiness instead of hiring someone else to do so. This was a step in the right direction.

"We have rules about birthday parties held at school." She smiled at him. "But what did you have in mind?"

Her sparkling eyes made him want to know what she had on her mind. The more time he spent with her, the more he wanted to spend. But he could think of better things to do than decorating a bulletin board. "Lots of things."

The husky way the words came out made it hard for Colly to think of birthday parties. "Like what?"

"Like you and me. Alone. On a moonlit island somewhere far away from finger paints and story time."

"That sounds more like a party for you than J.J." She laughed to force the image out of her thoughts. "Be serious."

"I am. If I invited you to a party like that, would you come?"

She almost gave him a resounding *yes* before she thought better of it. Instead she took a deep breath and said, "Ask me next spring."

"Why wait?"

"Because your birthday isn't until May. The issue we were discussing is J.J.'s birthday. So, what are your plans?"

"I thought about bringing in some ponies, maybe a couple of clowns or a magician. The usual stuff."

The usual stuff. "If that's the kind of party J.J. wants you'll have to have it somewhere else."

"That's what he said. I'll make sure the pony trainers clean up after the animals if that's what you're worried..." James's words trailed away when he saw the look on her face.

He knew his next suggestion would appeal to her kooky nature. "Okay, no animals. I have a friend with a hot-air balloon. I'm sure he could be persuaded to give all the kids a ride."

"James, be serious. Where would he land, in the street?"

"Nah, I can see that wouldn't work. How about if I rent one of those moon-walk things that the kids like to bounce on and have it set up out back?"

She shook her head. "You can't do any of those things here."

This was the first birthday celebration that James had ever been responsible for planning for his son and he wanted to make it one to remember. "Why not?"

"I can't allow such extravagant gestures here because they would point out the inequity of the children's parents' financial resources. It wouldn't be fair."

"Haven't you heard? Life is rarely ever fair. The kids are sure to notice those differences some day, you know."

"True, but they won't encounter them here. If you choose to hold that kind of party, it'll have to be away from the school."

"But J.J. doesn't have many friends and I don't want him to feel rejected if nobody shows up. I thought it would be better to hold it while they're already assembled."

"A captive audience?"

"Well, yes. J.J. wants a celebration with his classmates."

"And that's fine, as long as you're content to bring a regulation cake, some ice cream and a few game prizes. If you want I'll come up with the games and help you serve."

He frowned. "That sounds kind of ho-hum to me."

"Children have an innate ability to make their own fun, James," she reminded him.

"I know, but I want this party to be special. Something J.J. can remember."

"You can't buy him friends, you know. He has to make them on his own. And he will, his social skills have already shown a lot of improvement."

It irritated James that Colly would accuse him of having such low motives. "I'm not trying to buy friends for my son, I just want him to have a great birthday. Like the ones I had when I was a kid. What's wrong with that?"

"Nothing. And I can't tell you how glad I am that you want the day to be special for him." Her goal suddenly didn't seem as far away as it once had. "But I think you can come up with something more imaginative than a big overpriced extravaganza."

He had a feeling she was trying to convey something important, but for the life of him he couldn't guess what it was. "Like what?"

"Well, maybe something small and intimate might be more to J.J.'s liking."

James shrugged. "I thought the motto for children's parties was the more the merrier."

"Tell me, what made your birthday parties special as a child? What do you remember most about them?"

He thought back on that long-ago time. "After Dad died, my mother was too busy, first with law school and then with her practice, to do much more than hire someone else to plan them. But they were always lavish affairs, regulation birthday cake notwithstanding."

"But what made them memorable?"

"Now that I think about it, I was a lot like J.J. when I was a kid. I was quiet, a loner. Since I didn't have any special friends, every kid in my class was invited to my parties. They all came, too. They all ate the fancy cake and rode the ponies, or swam in the pool, or enjoyed the magician or whatever entertainment had been provided. We all had a high old time."

"Isn't there one thing that stands out in your memory?" she persisted.

What stood out in his memory was that at school on Monday, the other kids went their own ways and lonely little James went his. All he'd gotten out of it were expensive presents and memories of being the birthday boy for a couple of hours. He couldn't tell Colly that.

"Presents?" he suggested tentatively.

"Be serious," Colly admonished.

"I can't remember back that far," he lied. "Suppose you tell me about birthdays you remember."

"Okay." She smiled. "When I was a little girl, my parents always let me choose how I wanted to spend my birthday."

J.J.'s interest in the baby lizards had dwindled somewhere along the line, and he ambled over. "What did you choose, Colly?"

"One year I wanted a picnic and kite flying."

"Did you get your wish?"

"Of course she did." James leaned against the science table. "Her parents got off pretty easy that time."

"Not really." Colly sat on the floor and folded up her long legs. "My birthday is February first. It's pretty cold in Colorado that time of year. Too cold for picnics and kite flying. But I have a wonderful family and they wanted to make me happy. We spent a whole week building the kite."

"A week?" James looked skeptical.

"Anticipation is part of the fun."

"Why didn't you just buy one?" J.J. asked.

"In the commune where I lived, we liked to be self-sufficient. That means we never bought anything we could make ourselves."

James still couldn't get used to her strange beginning in life. But it seemed to have had a positive effect on the outcome.

"What's a commune?" J.J. wanted to know.

"It's a place where people gather together to live close to nature." It was a simplistic answer, but Colly didn't think J.J. was ready for a discussion of the collective ownership and use of property.

"Oh," James said. "Like the Indians back in the old days?"

"Sort of," she agreed.

"Tell us the rest of your birthday story. I like kites."

"We had a great time working on that kite together. Lots of people in the community helped. It was every color of the rainbow."

"It sounds great," J.J. enthused.

Colly grinned sheepishly. "It was. In the truest sense of the word. We got sort of carried away and made the thing so big we couldn't get it through the door."

"What did you do?" J.J. asked, wide-eyed.

"My dad had to take some of it apart to get it outside."

"Did you get to fly it your own self? I never did that before."

"I've never done that before," James automatically corrected, and wished he'd thought of flying a kite with his son.

"You neither, Dad?"

"It's been years since I've tried." James felt his old inadequacy creeping up on him again.

Colly recognized the self-doubt that flickered across his handsome face. "I'll teach you, J.J. I happen to be an expert."

"That's what I wanna do on my birthday!" he said. "Okay, Dad? Can we have a picnic and fly a kite on my birthday like Colly did? Just us three?"

"Wouldn't you like to invite someone your own age, J.J.?" she asked.

"I'll invite David, he's already five, but he's close to my age. Can we?"

James considered the request. Learning the art of kite flying might be fun, especially when the teacher was so pretty. "If Colly's agreeable, I certainly am."

Colly smiled at J.J.'s enthusiasm. Why had she told that story? And why had she offered to teach them how to fly a kite? This particular cause was becoming far too personal and she was spending entirely too much time with James and J.J. Where was emotional detachment when she needed it?

The Townsends were waiting for her answer. She knew she should try to keep some professional distance between them, but she couldn't disappoint J.J. "It sounds like a wonderful way to celebrate your birthday."

"Yippee!" J.J. was the only one who cheered. James watched her speculatively. Like a cat watches a canary cage. A patient man, he would wait until someone left the cage door open.

She wanted to tell him to go fly a kite. Unfortunately, she already had.

Chapter Four

J.J.'s birthday was on a convenient Sunday, which turned out to be a perfect day for flying kites in the park. It was a red and gold autumn day, full of sunshine and falling leaves and enough wind to make the enterprise worthwhile.

James arranged everything. He picked up David and Colly and the group arrived at Lincoln Park at ten in the morning. That gave them a couple of hours for kiting before they stopped to enjoy the picnic lunch packed by a local restaurant. Afterward, if the boys became bored with the kite or, heaven forbid, it wouldn't fly, James had a contingency plan. They could go on to the zoo or the Kirkpatrick Museum for diversion. He had all bases covered.

Or so he'd thought. So far nothing had gone according to his schedule. It had taken eight hands and two hours just to assemble the darn kite he'd purchased, and it still wouldn't fly. After reading and rereading the "simple" directions, James was beginning to think they'd done something wrong.

"I thought you said you were an expert kite flyer," he accused Colly with a grin.

"I think *were* is the operative word. Besides, my experience was limited to kites of the homemade variety." She surveyed the complicated, aerodynamically unsound specimen at her feet. "I've never even seen a kite like this before."

Neither had James. It was made of some space-age nylon and shaped like a dragon. It looked more like an overgrown 3-D wind sock than a kite. He looked at the crumpled dragon and wished he'd bought a regulation paper, triangle-shaped kite.

"The guy at the store told me this was the Mercedes-Benz of plane-surfaced kites and that it would practically fly itself. So why won't it fly?"

"Gravity?" Colly suggested with a muffled laugh. It was a joke he didn't find funny. "Maybe you should have asked him for the magic word."

J.J. giggled. "He said *dude* about a million times, maybe that's the magic word."

"That's what I get for trusting a teenage salesman," James grumbled.

"It's pretty wiggly," J.J. pointed out. "Maybe that's why it won't fly." His little friend David nodded a solemn agreement.

"Now, don't get discouraged," Colly told them with a dimpled grin. "All any kite needs is wind and we have plenty of that. Your dad and I will get it up, never fear."

James gave her a sassy wink. "We may even fly the kite, too."

She jabbed him in the ribs with her elbow and gave him a you-shouldn't-say-such-things glare. She took the questionable kite in hand and prepared to launch it again. "James, when the wind catches it be sure to let out more string this time."

"You always get the easy job," he teased. "Why don't you operate the string this trip and I'll run alongside you carrying this monstrosity."

"Hauling that wiggly beast isn't as simple as it looks," she argued good-naturedly.

"Mr. Townsend?" David tugged on James's hand. "Want me to do the string part for ya?" In a stage whisper directed at J.J., he added, "My dad can't ever get it up, either."

Colly didn't dare look at James so she pretended to check the wind velocity.

Consciously wiping the grin from his face, James said, "You know, the only people who can open child-proof containers are children. Let's turn it over to the kids, they'll have this thing flying in no time."

David nodded eagerly. Evidently he'd been working on a plan of his own. "J.J., you take the kite and we'll run up that hill over there and then run down this side. That oughta do it."

James and Colly handed over the kite and string. Having already proven themselves inept, they sat down on the blanket to watch the boys.

Practically dragging the kite between them, the children charged up a nearby knoll, shouted "Dude!" at the top of their lungs, and charged down. The fickle wind snapped at the nylon and flung the smiling dragon aloft. The brightly colored kite dipped and weaved as David played out the string. Finally, a gust caught it and it soared high overhead. Within minutes, the little boys had accomplished what the grown-ups had been attempting to do for hours.

After a moment of incredulity, Colly and James applauded the boys' efforts, calling out encouragement but no instructions. The kids didn't need their help at all. Finally they lapsed into an easy silence filled with the sounds of children's laughter and the occasional popping of the nylon kite.

"J.J. is really beginning to blossom," she said after a while. "He's speaking out in class and isn't afraid to voice his opinions these days."

"I'm glad he doesn't cry at school anymore. That always bothered me the most, like I'd let him down or something."

"Actually, he hasn't cried since his first day at Shady Dell. Have you noticed a difference in his attitude at home?"

"Yes," was all he said.

"Well?"

"Well what?"

"Don't just leave it at that. Tell me more."

James shrugged. "Little things. As you mentioned, he volunteers information instead of waiting to be asked. I'm hardly inside the house these days before he begins telling about his day. He never used to do that. He's not so shy about initiating hugs or other shows of affection. I think he's beginning to like me."

Colly smiled at the surprise in his voice. "Well, of course he does."

"I know he loves me, I'm his father. Children love their parents, but they don't necessarily have to *like* them."

"I see what you're getting at." She nodded, wondering if he felt that way about his own mother. "You're beginning to enjoy him more, too, aren't you?"

"Yeah, it's fun to come home now. I probably shouldn't admit this, but when J.J. first came to stay with me I was sometimes resentful. That's a terrible way to feel about your own child, isn't it?"

He looked so guilty. He'd suffered more uncertainty than she'd thought. "Maybe it wasn't J.J. you resented, but the situation. Your ex-wife placed you in a difficult position when she left without warning. You felt you were losing control and you resented that."

James gave her an odd look. "Yes, that's exactly it. But how did you know?"

Colly knew better than to mention astrology again. A Taurus man would never accept that his behavior might be predictable to others. "It must have been all those counseling courses I took."

He nodded. "I never thought I'd say this, but now there are days I resent having to go to work."

Her heart swelled with happiness for him and the little boy who would benefit from this new paternal affection. "That's wonderful, James."

"I still make mistakes and I worry that J.J. will suffer for them. But I don't worry as much as I did a month ago."

"Nobody's perfect, especially parents."

"I know, but you don't get do-overs where children are concerned. There are so many things I wish I'd done differently."

"He just turned five, you have your whole lives ahead of you."

"It's only a matter of time until Lenore comes back. When she does, I'm afraid I'll slip back into the weekend-parent category."

Colly glanced at him. "Have you heard from her?"

James nodded. "She called me at the office yesterday."

"Did she say when she was coming back?"

"I didn't really give her a chance. I lit into her, gave her hell for leaving the way she did. All she said in her defense was that it wasn't easy being a single parent and that it was time *I* faced up to my responsibilities."

"What does she plan to do about her own?"

"She didn't say." He shrugged. "Nothing for the time being, I suppose."

"You and J.J. have come a long way in the past few weeks, but I think you both need more time together."

James thought the same thing, but he'd been brainwashed by the popular notion that children were almost always better off with their mothers. He voiced that opinion.

"Things are changing," she told him. "There's no reason fathers can't be just as nurturing as mothers. Recent decisions by the courts have shown that view and have finally accepted what researchers have been saying for years. Have you given any thought to seeking permanent custody?"

"I've thought about it, sure. But I haven't made a decision."

"What's holding you back?"

"The thought that whatever I do will affect J.J. for the rest of his life. Making the wrong decision could be far worse than making none at all."

"Look at him," J.J. and David were still playing with the kite, their interest thoroughly engaged. "He seems like a happy, well-adjusted child. I couldn't have said that a month ago. You must be doing something right."

James watched his son. J.J. was running and laughing, having a great time. The other children from the park had joined in the fun and J.J. was the center of attention. In the spirit of cooperation, he gave each child a turn holding the kite string.

"Like most kids, he's adapted to the situation. I'm not sure I can take credit for his adaptability."

Colly stared at her hands for a moment. "I'd like to ask you a rather personal question."

He gave her his full attention. For weeks he'd been trying his best to get personal with her, and even though she seemed to gravitate toward him, she always managed to keep him at an emotional distance.

"Fire away."

She turned the full force of her gaze on him. "What will really happen when Lenore comes back?"

James sighed. Leaning on one hand, he ran his finger down the length of her jaw. "Absence has not made my heart grow fonder, if that's what you're getting at. Just the opposite, in fact."

"Are you sure there's no chance the two of you could work things out? Not even for J.J.'s sake?"

It went against his nature to confide his private life, but unlike other women he had known, Colly was easy to talk to. He needed her understanding and wanted to explain everything. He'd never felt that way before. He turned away from her, his gaze once more searching for his son.

He spotted him and visibly relaxed. "There's no chance of that happening. We both had second thoughts before the ink was dry on the wedding invitations. When I voiced my concerns Lenore told me about the baby. I cared about her and I wanted to do the honorable thing, but you have to understand that we both knew we were off to a shaky start. We hoped things would get better between us but they just went from bad to worse.

"We tried to make it work and it did for a while. We cared, but deep down we didn't understand each other. We didn't want the same things."

"So you buried yourself in your business?" she guessed.

"That's one way to put it. Lenore buried herself in credit cards and tried to buy happiness. When the fun of that wore off, she turned to new friends. It wasn't long before she met someone else. The divorce was a mutual decision. If it hadn't been for J.J., it wouldn't have been particularly painful."

"Did you meet someone, too?" she asked quietly.

"I was too busy to look. After the divorce I met women, but none of them were special." He refrained from adding, "Until I met you."

Colly knew her initial opinion of James had been wrong. He wasn't ambitious and self-involved because he didn't care about anyone else, but because he cared too much. "Why hasn't Lenore remarried?"

"I never asked." Talking about his failures always dampened his mood. "I guess it has something to do with forfeiting alimony."

Colly told herself that concern for J.J. was the reason she was asking so many questions. But something had gone wrong, her feelings for James had gotten tangled up with the ones she had for his son. She'd do well to stop this line of questioning because his answers were becoming too important to her. After all, her interest was strictly that of a teacher for a pupil. Wasn't it?

She avoided meeting James's gaze by watching the drift of cotton ball clouds overhead. There was one more question she had to ask. "Do you think you'll marry again?"

James cupped her chin in his fingers and turned her face until their gazes met. He looked into her green eyes and wondered if he was falling in love. "Yes," he whispered, dipping his head slightly until his lips were mere inches from her own. "I do."

It was a gentle kiss, but it sent the pit of her stomach into a wild whirl and made Colly yearn for more. She leaned into him and clasped her arms around his neck, kissing him back with unexpected fervor.

His hands slid around her waist, pulling her more fully into his embrace. When his lips covered hers hungrily and his tongue explored the innermost recesses of her mouth, Colly was transported to a place where nothing, and no one else existed.

There was only James. His mouth on hers made her forget things she shouldn't; his hands on her neck and shoulders made her want to feel them in forbidden places.

"Hey, Dad," J.J. called excitedly, as the boys galloped toward them. "This is fun!"

Colly hastily pulled away from James, shocked by her overly eager response. She smoothed her hair and pretended a sudden interest in the picnic basket.

James had completely lost himself in the caress and his voice was abnormally husky when he called out to his son.

"It's great, J.J." He leaned toward Colly and in an aside that only she could hear, he added, "And that kiss was pretty terrific, too."

"Yes," she agreed as she removed a container of pickles. "But it's still a bad idea."

"You're right, and I promise to try to exhibit more restraint when there are children around."

"I'd appreciate that."

"I can't promise you I won't take advantage of the opportunity when they aren't."

"James, can't you accept the fact that we're destined to be friends and nothing else?"

"No, I can't accept that. You're very special to me, Colly."

She sighed. "That's because I've taken an interest in J.J."

"It's more than that," he said softly. "Much more."

"If you were completely honest with yourself, you'd realize—"

"I'm taking an awful chance in confessing this because I don't think you're ready to hear it. But I've never felt so...so tender toward a woman before. I didn't know I could feel this way."

James's confession left Colly momentarily speechless. Maybe she should tell him the truth before things got out of hand. But what was the truth? That she was only seeing him to insure the happiness of her student? If *she* were completely honest, she'd have to admit it was much more than that.

She chose her words carefully. "I feel a special tenderness for you, too, but that sometimes happens in a situation like ours."

James smiled. "And what situation would that be?"

"Well—" she paused, hoping to phrase it as delicately as possible. She kept her gaze on the pickles. "We like each other and we have something very important in common. We share a mutual desire."

"I'm glad to hear that."

She tried to ignore his remark, but her stomach fluttered anyway. "A desire to make J.J. happy."

"I hope you'll feel the same way about me once you get to know me better."

His happiness was becoming as important to her as
J.J.'s and that's what worried her. Before she could say
more, James called the boys over to lunch. Their hair was
plastered to their heads with baby sweat and they were
breathless when they plopped down on the blanket. Their
wide eyes grew wider as James unpacked the cooler.

"What's that goopy black stuff?" J.J. asked suspi-
ciously.

"Caviar," his father informed him.

"But what is it?" J.J. queried.

"Fish eggs," Colly said with a smothered grin.

"I don't want any," David announced.

"Me neither," J.J. added.

"Have you guys ever tasted it?" James asked patiently.

"No way," the boys cried in unison.

"Then you don't know what you're missing. Do they,
Colly?"

"I believe it's an acquired taste. One I haven't quite
developed myself."

James shrugged and tossed the jar back into the cooler.
"So much for that appetizer. We still have plenty of other
goodies in here." He pulled out a foam platter wrapped
in see-through plastic.

"Now that's more like it," Colly said with enthusiasm. "Good old-fashioned deviled eggs."

"Can I have one?" David asked Colly. "I already had
eggs for breakfast."

"I'm glad I had cereal 'cause I love debbiled eggs,"
J.J. said.

James shook his head. "I've never met such diet-
conscious five-year-olds."

"We've been learning about Clara Cholesterol this
week," Colly told him.

James smiled and took out another platter. "How do you feel about fried chicken, David?"

"Yum, yum!" David licked his lips and patted his tummy.

James raised an eyebrow at Colly.

"Freddie Fat is next week," she explained. "Is there any potato salad in that cooler?"

"What, no inhibitions about Connie Carbohydrate?" James delved into the cooler again. "I was afraid to bring it out."

The boys laughed. "There are good carbos and bad," J.J. explained. "Potatoes are good."

When they'd all eaten their fill, James unveiled the birthday cake. It was decorated with colorful kites and proclaimed "Happy Birthday J.J." in bright blue frosting letters. After the traditional song, James lit the five candles.

"Make a wish, J.J., and don't tell anyone," Colly encouraged him. "If you blow out all the candles, your wish will come true."

He closed his eyes, puffed out his little cheeks and blew as hard as he could.

"You got 'em all, J.J.," David cheered.

"With a little help from the wind," James teased.

J.J.'s forehead wrinkled in thought. "Do you think my wish will come true if the wind helped?"

James hurried to reassure his son. "Of course, it's your birthday."

"Yippee!" He clapped his hands.

James helped him cut and serve the cake. He knew what he wished for—that this feeling of contentment would last forever.

As it turned out, they didn't need the zoo for diversion. They played on the swings and slides in the park, the children challenging the grown-ups to a high-swinging contest. Finally, late in the afternoon, they delivered a very sleepy David home to his parents. J.J. was asleep in the backseat by the time they pulled up in Colly's driveway.

Colly had been waiting on the porch for them when they arrived that morning, and James had yet to see the inside of her house. He suspected it was as quirky as she was, but it appeared he wouldn't find out today.

"There's no need to get out," she told him. "I know you don't like leaving J.J. alone in the car."

He checked the sleeping child. "Can we sit on the porch for a few minutes? We have some unfinished business," James said, helping Colly out of the car and leading her to the porch.

"Like what?"

"Like this," he said in a husky voice, his head descending toward hers.

Colly had no chance to think before he kissed her. By the time the tip of his tongue traced the outline of her lips, she was past thinking. Her arms slid around his neck and she gave herself up to the moment. His tongue swept inside her mouth, hot and persuasive.

His hands caught her hips and pulled her against him. He moved his hips against hers, rocking gently, a lazy motion that matched his questing tongue. Colly was lost to the passion that claimed her.

"I had to do this just one more time before I left," he murmured against her cheek.

She moved in his arms, enjoying the feel of his hard chest against her soft one. One of his arms tightened around her waist while his other hand massaged her hip.

He ended the kiss, but he wasn't through with her yet. His lips caressed her cheek, her eyelids and her jaw. He nibbled gently at her ear. "I can't stand this much longer, Colly. Will you go out with me?"

Shaken by the intensity of his words, Colly asked breathlessly, "Out where?"

Without losing the warmth of bodily contact, he leaned his head back and smiled. "To dinner, a movie, a concert, Lover's Leap. Anywhere. As long as we're together, alone."

"Like a date?"

He kissed the tip of her nose. "Something like that."

She backed out of his arms so she could think more clearly. "Without J.J.?"

He chuckled. "Definitely without J.J."

She turned her back to him and unlocked the door. "I thought J.J. was the reason we've been spending time together." There, she had admitted the truth at last. Sort of.

"I know you're worried about ethics, but we can be discreet."

"I don't like the sound of that."

"It's foolish for us to continue denying what we both feel. Don't you agree?" He reached for her but she quickly stepped inside.

"I'm sorry, but I can't." She shut the door and leaned against it.

James's voice penetrated the thick wood. "I'm not giving up, Colly."

No, she didn't think he would. Bulls were a model of patience. Especially when they wanted something.

What did she want? To open the door and fling herself into his arms? Or to exercise caution? James aroused her as no man ever had. He tapped feelings she'd never known before. But how long would it last? Colly knew herself pretty well. As soon as J.J. was permanently in

James's custody her goal would be reached, her job would be done. She'd go on to the next project. It had happened before. Her emotions were fickle and it could happen again.

Not fickle in a bad way, she told herself. Luz said she had a short attention span. Men never seemed to stay in her affections for long. The more time she spent with them, the more boring they ultimately became.

It occurred to her that if her reasoning was correct, the only way to stop thinking about James was to spend more time with him. It sounded perverse, but it might work. If he persisted in his pursuit, she'd comply. That way their amazing chemistry could play itself out.

"You're too stubborn for your own good, James," she said aloud, unsure if he was still out there.

"Not stubborn," he replied. "Determined."

She heard his steps as he left the porch and breathed a deep sigh of relief. A cool shower and an early night would help her see things straight.

Later, she lay in bed unable to sleep. Uninvited memories of James's lips intruded, leaving her feeling restless and wanting. She turned on the light and on the bedside table noticed a new astrology magazine she'd bought the day before. She flipped the pages until she found her horoscope for the month.

"The private you has a hundred schemes going and that's why you present that preoccupied facade to friends, family and lovers."

Lovers? James was the only man who had ever come close to fitting that description, but anything was possible.

"But a facade is all it is! True, you can be distracted—Aquarius is the sign of the visionary—but there is a side of you that craves intimacy, too."

James was the only man who had aroused the craving.

"There are not many men who hold your easily diverted attention long enough to reassure the hidden you. Even fewer men last long enough to experience your hidden passions."

"That's true," she mused with a laugh. "Until tonight, there hadn't even been one."

"But just when you're ready to give up the search, Mr. Wonderful steps in. He's handsome, fun, sexy and honorable. However, he might be a bit of a workaholic like you. The path to togetherness is not without the proverbial rocks. In fact, there will be times it could be called the pits. Is it worth the trouble? You bet!"

Colly flung the magazine to the floor. She'd wasted her money. It wasn't based on real astrology, but rather on the fantasies of lonely women. The person who'd written that mumbo jumbo didn't know beans about Aquarians.

Chapter Five

A few weeks later, Colly was talking to the Townsends'
housekeeper and learned that James had given the older
woman four days off for Thanksgiving. Brigit wanted to
spend the holiday with her daughter in Tulsa, but was
concerned that James and J.J. would have to eat the traditional turkey dinner alone in a restaurant. To ease Brigit's mind, and her own, Colly invited them to spend the
day with her at her parents' home.

James had indeed been determined. He'd asked her out
at least once a week since J.J.'s birthday but she'd laugh-
ingly turned him down each time. Now she was inviting
him to meet her parents, a fact that Luz had found mar-
velously ironic. But it wasn't a date, Colly told herself, it
was a good deed.

James eagerly accepted her invitation. It wouldn't be
the intimate dinner he'd hoped for, but at least they'd be
together, which was more than he could say for the past
few weeks. He'd attended each and every one of the par-

ent meetings at school, he'd sat in on group pep talks covering topics from bed-wetting to sibling rivalry. He'd put in his weekly allotment of hours and then some. But they hadn't been alone.

He'd asked her out often, but Colly had turned him down every time. Talk about stubborn. Her integrity and scruples were starting to get in the way. The unexpected invitation to accompany her to her parents' was a surprise, but he had no inclination to question it. He just wanted to enjoy the time they would spend together.

On Thanksgiving he and J.J. set out for the Fairchild home. The house had been built before statehood and was located on a lovely old block in a historic area of the city. Like many of its turn-of-the-century neighbors, it had been lovingly restored to its former glory. The muted pastel paint and white trim of the grand old homes brightened the dreary gray landscape.

The stage was currently set for a snowstorm of one or more acts, but the empty flower gardens, abandoned gazebos, leafless oaks and frost-killed lawns promised graciousness when spring returned to Oklahoma.

Glancing at his watch, James noted that they were right on time, eleven o'clock. He parked on the street and ushered J.J. up to the front door where warm light spilled through leaded glass side panels. He made a hurried dab at the overlooked milk mustache on his son's upper lip and lifted the heavy brass knocker. In a moment the door swung open and Colly's welcoming smile took the chill out of the air.

She was dressed in a loden green wool skirt and matching cashmere sweater set, complete with gold-tone sweater clip. Her curling hair was caught back in a loose French braid revealing tiny pearl earrings. Her heavy stockings were also green as were her flat loafers. As always, the effect was dramatic; today she was an elfin sprite doing a fair imitation of a fifties-era Bryn Mawr coed.

She looked so cute and vulnerable that he wanted to sweep her into his arms. But he had to settle for a peck on the cheek, identical to the one she gave his son. After a comment about the weather, Colly led them into the kitchen to meet her family.

James had a brief impression of high ceilings, tall windows, shiny oak floors and beautiful antiques as he followed Colly through the house. The kitchen, which was full of copper pans and mouth-watering aromas, was larger than the living room in his condo. It was crowded with laughing people busily preparing what promised to be a feast.

Everyone greeted Colly and her guests as she led James and J.J. to a kitchen island where a couple was filling tart shells with cranberry mousse, assembly-line style.

"Mom, Dad, I'd like you to meet my friend James Townsend and his son J.J."

James smiled at the appellation. Maybe they were merely friends in Colly's mind, but if he had his way, they would soon be much more. He turned to the couple and was so startled that he was a bit slow to shake their proffered hands. He'd assumed the young man and woman were Colly's friends; he never would have guessed they were her parents.

During the introductions, Peter Fairchild draped a protective arm across his daughter's shoulders. Like Colly, he was tall and slender. His patrician good looks were those of an artist or poet. He was dressed in a blue silk shirt, stylishly faded jeans and boots. His wild blond mane was worn shoulder length, but there was nothing feminine about the hair or the man. James knew he had to be in his early forties, but his long face was unlined and he appeared no older than James himself.

Colly's mother, Pamela, was also tall and boyishly slim. Her brown hair was shaped into a pixie cap that hugged her pretty face and emphasized expressive blue eyes filled with warmth. The ruffled plaid pinafore apron she wore over a sleek red jersey dress enhanced her youthful appearance.

Pamela welcomed them into her home and graciously accepted the flowers and wine James offered.

"I never would have taken you for Colly's mother," he complimented her honestly.

"People often mistake us for sisters," Mrs. Fairchild admitted modestly. "I tell them I was a child bride." With a saucy wink that was very much like Colly's, she turned back to her tart making.

Next, Colly introduced James and J.J. to her younger brothers. The boys were supposed to be shining silver flatware but they were using the cutlery in a mock battle instead. Their actions drew good-natured reprimands and what's-the-use looks from their parents.

Raven, whose fair coloring made his name a misnomer, was a high school senior intent on an acting career. His style of dress was as dramatic as his sister's, and James suspected the young man would feel very much at home on a stage.

Skye, a skinny twelve-year-old in baggy skater pants, offered to teach J.J. how to play his latest video game. He was obviously eager to escape, either the polishing chores or his brother, and as soon as James nodded his approval, the two boys scampered off.

The Fairchild home was crowded with aunts, uncles, cousins and friends. Some clustered around the televised football game in the den, others huddled over a game board in the living room. The kitchen was standing room only with cooks, kibitzers and hangers-on who hoped to sample the delicious food being prepared.

Blissfully unaware of their noisy surroundings, babies napped in playpens and travel beds, which provided tranquil islands in the constant stream of humanity. Children, chased by an odd assortment of pets, clattered through the house playing their own mysterious games.

Colly introduced James to the rest of the guests, and sensing his discomfort, led him out to the atrium to escape the crowd. "Peace and quiet," she whispered with a grin. "Make the most of it while you can."

James took her at her word and stole a kiss that, though short, was as warm and sultry as the air in the atrium.

"That wasn't exactly what I had in mind." The kiss had been a pleasant surprise. It had also made her want more. "Is that the best you can do?" she teased. "After all, it's a holiday."

Now it was James's turn to be surprised. He saw the invitation in her eyes and pulled her into his arms for a more thorough version. Like Colly, the kiss was sweet and dreamy.

"Is that better?" he asked.

"Much. But it makes me nervous to kiss you in my parents' house."

"It makes me a little nervous, too," he admitted and backed away. "You know, I still can't get over how young your parents are."

"They were only eighteen when I was born," she reminded him.

He frowned. "Oh, yeah. I keep forgetting how young *you* are."

His words served to remind her of the disparity in their life experiences and she pretended interest in a verdant rubber plant while trying to sort out her thoughts.

Sometimes James forgot all about their seven-year age difference. When he held her he forgot about damn near everything. But at times like this, he had to wonder what he was doing, getting mixed up with an unconventional young woman like Colly. They'd seemed friendly, but how could her parents approve of her seeing a divorced man with a child? Maybe she'd told them they were just friends.

Maybe that's all they ever would be.

"We'd better go back to the kitchen where it's safe," he suggested.

"Coward."

"Maybe, but I think it's best."

"What's wrong?" she asked.

"I'd hate for your parents to think I'm a dirty old man."

She laughed. "My parents are open-minded."

"They seem very protective of you."

"They've always encouraged me to be independent, but they're interested in everything I do. I guess we're close because we practically grew up together."

It was hard for James to understand such family ties. His mother lived in Dallas, and though it was only a few hours away their contacts were limited to twice-yearly visits and calls on birthdays and Mother's Day. She'd recently married her law partner and she and her husband were too busy litigating to have time for family togetherness. His own schedule had kept him from feeling he'd missed anything. So why was he thinking about it now? He was loathe to admit it, but all this warmth made him uncomfortable.

"I've never been part of a real family unit. I don't remember my father and my mother didn't have time for festivities." He didn't add that his mother had thought it silly to cook Thanksgiving dinner for two people. His childhood memories involved restaurants, not reunions.

"You must have been a lonely little boy," Colly observed.

"I'm not complaining, mind you," he asserted. "Mother always made sure I had everything I needed."

"Everything except herself?" she guessed.

"She loved me," he said softly. "I just wasn't her top priority. I can't help noticing the difference between your family and mine. Thanks for inviting us here today and for giving J.J. the chance to be a part of things. At least he'll have a pleasant holiday memory."

"Don't you have any?" she asked gently.

He thought for a moment then grinned. "I remember one Thanksgiving when I was ten or so. Mother was busy working on a brief for a big case and forgot all about eating. I watched the Macy's parade on TV and then went to my room so I wouldn't disturb her. About six o'clock I got hungry and tapped on her door. She was up to her eyeballs in deposition notes and actually seemed surprised to see me.

"When I reminded her that it was Thanksgiving, she apologized and sent me to get dressed up to go out. All we could find open at that hour was a Chinese restaurant. We had a very non-traditional Thanksgiving dinner of egg rolls and moo shu pork. For a little while, she seemed to forget about her case and lavished all her attention on me. It was the most fun we'd had together in a long time."

James laughed, but Colly sensed the underlying regret in his words. She also better understood why he was so uncomfortable in a nurturing role; he'd had so little experience with the kind of loving attention she'd always taken for granted. It saddened her to think of him growing up without benefit of involved parents, but it saddened her even more to think of J.J. doing so.

She was convinced, even more than before, that hers was an important mission. J.J. needed the kind of father James could be, but James needed help fulfilling his role. Help that she could provide.

After a big midday meal that seemed to go on and on, course after course, Colly showed James to a quiet bedroom where they settled a sleepy J.J. down for a nap. They tiptoed into the hall and she suggested they go for a walk.

"Shouldn't we help clean up?" he asked.

"Are you kidding? They have dozens of hands, no one will miss ours. Besides, the football fans have committed to that."

The sky was leaden but the snow had missed its cue. Nonetheless, they bundled up warmly in coats and gloves to protect them against the chill.

"This is a charming neighborhood," James said after they'd passed several renovated houses. He reached out, slipped off her mitten, removed his own glove and tucked their clasped hands into his coat pocket.

Colly's heart raced a little at the innocent yet intimate gesture. James's hand was incredibly warm and the feel of his skin against hers, even if it was only his hand, was a delightful sensation.

She forced her attention back to the conversation. "When we moved here ten years ago, only a few homes had been reclaimed. Some were empty and some were badly in need of repairs. Everyone wanted to move to the suburbs. But when Mom and Dad started working on our house the improvements they made excited interest in the neighborhood. Some of their artist friends bought houses they wouldn't have considered before. They were amazed at the miracles a little elbow grease could perform.''

"And a lot of money," he put in.

"That, too. Mom and Dad formed a restoration association and eventually got the whole block listed on the National Registry of Historic Homes."

"It sounds like a big investment in time and money."

"Preserving the past is worth it," she declared.

"Your interest in the past is surprising in one so young." But then, she was often full of surprises.

"I've thought about that. About why I like old clothes, old houses, old jewelry—"

"Old men?" he teased.

"You're not so ancient." She snuggled against his side and squeezed his hand.

"So tell me, why do you like old things?"

"I think I was influenced as a child. My parents and Professor always made me feel like I was part of a long chain. An important element in the universe. I've always thought of the present as a continuance of the past. Dressing in the styles and collecting the furniture of other periods allows me to be a part of times I never knew."

"What about the future?"

"The future is a continuance of the present. Things just go on forever, with each age and each culture contributing something important."

"Very philosophical. In my business, I can't afford to spend much time thinking about the meaning of the universe."

"Of course not, you're a Taurus. I, on the other hand, am an Aquarian. You're rooted to earth and I'm always buzzing around somewhere in the stars." At his skeptical look, she continued. "I know you don't believe in sun signs and astrology and the rest of it, but it's true. From the moment of our births, we're all set on certain life courses whether you like it or not."

"I prefer to think each individual sets his own course," he disagreed. "We get out of life what we put into it in terms of hard work and dedication. We captain our own destiny."

"Spoken like a true Taurus," she said with a twinkling smile.

"What's that mean?"

"It means you're too stubborn to see anyone's viewpoint but your own. And I mean that in the kindest way."

"Excuse me if I feel insulted," he bantered. "I am not stubborn. I'm patient."

"You're hardheaded," she insisted.

"I am not. I'm sensible. Determined. There's a big difference."

"Whatever you say. Taurus men like to be the boss," she added airily as they approached a small park. A few wooden benches were set under leafless oaks. In the playground area, swings and slides stood in disuse, waiting for warmer weather and the laughing children who would seek their pleasure under the shady branches. Colly pulled James over to the swing set. Their shoes crunched in the pebbles spread beneath them.

"You push," she ordered as she settled herself on the sling-type seat. "As high as it'll go."

Still concerned over her last remarks, James complied. Did he really like to be the boss? Didn't he have to be? He wondered what his employees would think if they saw their workaholic leader frolicking in a winter-bound park. No doubt they'd assume his punishing schedule had finally tipped him over the edge.

"Higher!" she called to him.

"Are you always such a thrill seeker?"

"Always."

"Then what are you doing hanging around with a stodgy, conservative *Taurus?*" he asked with an emphasis on the last word.

"Don't you know? I'm trying to corrupt you."

He stepped around the swing to see her better and watched her fly through the air, her long braid like a banner behind her. Her slim legs flexed and extended as she propelled herself. The funny green socks and shoes didn't seem so funny now, but were somehow endearing. As endearing as the woman herself.

She'd been kidding about the corruption part, of course. Given half a chance, it was he who would corrupt her. How could anyone be as wise and as innocent as Columbine Fairchild?

The swing slowed and she jumped off, the momentum carrying her into his arms. James held her tightly, filled with a rush of emotion. Before he could think about it, his lips lowered to hers and held them in a kiss whose heat was defense against the cold air around them. It took little urging for him to deepen the kiss, to explore the warmth of her mouth with his tongue. He clasped her to him, his hand finding the thick rope of her braid, holding it as a drowning man would hold a lifeline. But it wasn't the sea that threatened to engulf him, it was the tempest of his own desire.

Colly reveled in James. In the tender tough kiss, in the pounding of his heart through his coat. His strength was exciting, his response passionate, but still she didn't understand this man she'd come to care about. Or was it J.J. who had touched her heart?

She was so absorbed in the moment and in the kiss that thoughts of the child surprised her. They also reminded her that maybe she'd taken this particular crusade too far. She slipped out of his embrace before she could forget herself entirely. "Maybe we should head back. It still looks like snow."

James was amazed at how quickly the topic had turned from passion to weather. He pretended to study the sky while his pulse settled into a normal rhythm. "I think you're right."

"James?"

"Yeah?"

"Thanks for the thrill."

He grinned. "The swing or the kiss?"

"Both."

They left the park and headed for the Fairchild home in the opposite direction from which they'd come. Both were silent and careful to keep their gloved hands to themselves, for fear that even slight contact would lead to another scorching kiss. After a few blocks, James turned to the neutral subject of Colly's family, a topic she seemed ever ready to discuss.

"I noticed the stained glass windows in the house. Did your parents make them?"

"Yes. Aside from the art in their gallery, they do custom work. They've created windows for a lot of churches and homes in the city. It's an old, intricate art but they're so talented they amaze me sometimes."

"You're very proud of them."

"Who wouldn't be? They're intelligent and totally devoted to each other. They've been married literally since they were children and I fully expect them to celebrate their seventy-fifth wedding anniversary. They're creative, loving and generous with their time and talent.

They're never too busy to help others and they've been great to me and my brothers. If I'd been allowed to choose, I would have picked them for my parents."

"So why did you move out on your own?" He wondered why she lived alone when her parents' home obviously had plenty of room.

"That's a silly question." She kicked at a windfall of russet oak leaves. "I needed a place to keep all my collections. My sweater clips alone were overrunning the joint."

"Seriously, Colly."

She sensed his need to know and wondered if it had anything to do with his own anxiety as a parent. "I love my family, but I have a life of my own. I believe in that old saying, the greatest gifts parents can give their children are roots and wings."

"It sounds simple, but it's hard to know how to be a good parent," he said earnestly.

"It's never simple. My experience with my pupils and their families has taught me that. There's no relationship more fragile or more enduring than that of parent and child. Or more complex."

"Life's been a roller coaster ever since J.J. came to live with me," he admitted. "When he was with his mother, he occupied an important place in my life, but it was just one little compartment—visitation. I could control the time we spent together because I knew that nothing I could do in those few hours could scar him or cause him lasting emotional damage."

"It was all fun," she interpreted.

"Well, yeah. We went to the zoo or the park, ate an ice cream, and I took him home. It was fun."

"But it wasn't reality."

He grinned wryly. "Hardly. When Lenore left and I was responsible for this little person, I realized what strangers we were. The truth is, we hardly knew each other."

"And now?"

"We're learning. It breaks my heart to disappoint him. He's so trusting, it tears me up to think I might fail him. And it hurts."

"What hurts?" she asked.

"Being a full-time father. J.J. has so many needs, sometimes I feel like he's eating me alive. Can you understand what I'm saying?"

"I understand. I've never had a child, but I know about their needs. Every one of my students takes a little piece of me. But they give so much more than they take. They teach me more than I could ever teach them."

When James looked at her she saw the confusion and uncertainty in his eyes. She wanted to reassure him, to tell him that everything would be all right, but she couldn't be dishonest. Despite her perpetually optimistic nature, she knew he and J.J. weren't all right yet.

She touched his wind-reddened cheek in a comforting gesture. "J.J. loves you," she said. That much she knew.

"For now, maybe. But what about tomorrow? What about all the tomorrows?"

"What about them, James? What are you doing to assure your future with him?"

"What can I do? Lenore has custody and I expect she'll turn up again, sooner or later. Once she's had her fun she'll want things to go back to the way they were before."

"Is that fair to J.J.? Or to you?"

"I don't know. I keep telling myself that a kid his age needs to be with his mother. That somehow she's better at nurturing him than I could ever be. Then I remember our marriage and I realize Lenore doesn't have it in her to nurture anyone.''

''I know we talked about this before, but maybe it's time for you to seriously consider obtaining custody,'' she suggested.

''That's all I have been thinking about lately. I'm just not sure it would be in J.J.'s best interests. I don't want to repeat the same mistakes my mother made with me.''

''I don't think you would,'' she told him sincerely. ''You've changed in the time I've known you. You can be exactly what J.J. needs.''

''Maybe I don't know how to be unselfishly dedicated to the happiness of another person.''

''You can learn.''

''Are you volunteering to teach me, teacher?''

Colly looked away. She couldn't tell him that she'd long since made up her mind to do just that. How presumptuous such an admission would sound. Hoping to divert his attention, she pointed out a For Sale sign in front of the house they were passing.

''That's what you need,'' she told him. ''A project.''

James smiled at the abrupt change of subject. He was getting used to the changes. He looked at the house, which was a forlorn old Victorian, sadly in need of a wrecking ball. ''That's not a project, that's a headache. I already have plenty of those, thank you.''

''All it needs is—''

''Someone out of his mind to spend a fortune on it,'' he finished for her.

''I was going to say, a little TLC. Our house was much worse than this when we started.''

"Really?" He didn't want to be interested, but he was. Memories of the warm Fairchild home made his current residence seem empty and austere.

"Really. Come on, let's see if we can look around inside."

Despite his protests that they were trespassing, they tried all the doors and even some of the windows, but could not gain entry.

"See what I mean?" she asked. "These places are solid as a rock. They don't build them like this anymore."

A few glimpses in windows had aroused James's curiosity. The ground floor had a wide veranda complete with columns. It had a round corner room that extended up to the second story, bow windows downstairs and dormers upstairs. Though somewhat worse for wear, the house possessed charm and a wealth of architectural details. The fact that it was still standing after ninety-odd years was testimony to the skill that had gone into its construction. Colly was right, they didn't build them like this anymore.

"Look at that fan window and those gables," she pointed out gleefully. "And the leaded glass and the oak floors and the gingerbread trim."

"And the leaky roof and the sagging steps and the peeling paint," he added with a grin.

"All minor details easily corrected. In the right hands, this house could be a showplace. What do you think? You said you might be in the market."

James had mentioned buying a house when he sold the condominium, but he'd been thinking of a move-in, owner-friendly place. This potential showplace could also be a potential disaster. "It would take too much work. It wouldn't be cost effective."

"Oh, pooh. You don't even know how much they're asking for it. You might get it for a song."

"I have a feeling that the song would be the blues."

"You're such a pessimist. Don't you have any imagination? Picture it with a fresh coat of colonial blue paint. White on the veranda and trim, of course. Some of Mom's and Dad's stained glass where those upper windows used to be. Hanging baskets of red geraniums and ferns at the windows. A glider on the veranda. Picture yourself in the glider drinking iced coffee."

He considered the tableau. The thought of having Colly at his side somehow made the whole project more palatable. "Are you sitting in the glider, too?"

"Maybe."

He laughed. "You and your imagination. All I see is surly contractors, missed deadlines, sawdust, and plumbing and wiring scenarios by Stephen King."

She sniffed. "You're so practical. So Taurean. J.J. needs a house as badly as this house needs a family."

"Too much work," he insisted, enjoying her earnest attempts to convince him.

"Since when," she asked, "is James Judson Townsend Sr. afraid of a little hard work?"

They were on the veranda and a sudden gust of wind whirled a flurry of autumn leaves around their legs like a miniature tornado. He reached for her as she leaned into him and their kiss was electrifying in its intensity. The wind rattled a pane of glass and the porch shuddered beneath them.

For an undreamed of moment, Colly's fantasies seemed real to James. As he tasted her sweetness he could almost believe in the idyllic life she had pictured. A life full of long summers and love, a life of cozy winters and family holidays. A life like the one Peter and Pamela Fairchild had together.

He'd never thought of himself in that kind of setting before. He'd never thought it was possible. But maybe with Colly he could create a strong family that would endure as this old house had endured.

As long as the kiss lasted, he could believe in the dream.

Almost.

Chapter Six

Before long it was time to replace the pilgrims and turkeys on the classroom bulletin board with fat Santas and Christmas trees. On the first day of December Colly arranged a new display on the low bookcase in front of the windows: a small sleigh pulled by little flocked reindeer. An antique wooden Santa sat in the driver's seat, but much to the children's dismay, the sleigh was empty.

She explained that for each of the next twenty-four days, they could find an old-fashioned toy hidden somewhere in the classroom. When all the toys were loaded into Santa's sleigh it would be Christmas Eve.

Not only did the activity increase their anticipation, but it provided a way for the children to count the days until Christmas. It also gave Colly a chance to teach them about holiday traditions and playthings of the past. Each day brought new delight as they discovered toys from her collection—lead soldiers, old teddy bears, rag dolls, tops, marbles, books and tiny tea sets. They were intrigued by the fanciful tales she spun about each item.

A few days later, James walked in at storytime. Luz, dressed in a practical uniform of jeans and sweater, motioned for him to take a seat at the back of the room. Impractical Colly was up front, radiant in a red woolen jumper from the forties. The sleek lines of the dress emphasized her small waist and long legs. Her seductive young body was almost always at odds with her wholesome good looks.

In keeping with her outfit, her hair was waved and rolled in a pompadour that Rosie the Riveter would have been proud of. Clamped to the back of her head was a silly little hat with a black feather that made him smile.

Ruffles frothed at the throat of her white blouse and faux rubies dangled from her ears. On anyone else the look would have been eccentric, but on Colly it was . . . just Colly. And that was enough.

She looked up to give him a smile of welcome, then went back to recounting the story of the Calico Cat and Gingham Dog. Faded and much-loved replicas of the story characters perched in her lap, waiting to be placed in Santa's sleigh.

The children were seated on a big blue carpet where they gathered for quiet activities. Colly called it the Magic Carpet and James could clearly see why. Her expressive voice and theatrical storytelling ability did indeed work magic over her young audience. As she regaled them with the story of the quarreling toys, little bodies stopped fidgeting and all eyes faced forward.

He spotted J.J. stretched out on his stomach, chin in his upturned palms. The child's concentration was intense and James wondered again how Colly did it. He could no more understand the power she had over the children than he could understand her power over him. He was as entranced by the pretty and unconventional teacher as was this room full of five-year-olds. And just as vulnerable to her charm.

He hadn't planned to be attracted to Colly and had tried his best to resist. But resistance was pointless. Hers was the kind of personality that snuck up on a man, beguiling him when he thought he was well past beguiling.

The more he learned about her, the more amazed he was by the contrasts in her personality. How could she be both whimsical child and wise woman? Sensible and eccentric, trusting and cautious, naive and manipulative, all at the same time? He sensed that loving Colly would be like opening a present every day.

He hadn't fully allowed himself that luxury and already her influence in his life was profound. Since Thanksgiving, he'd found himself rearranging his busy schedule so that he could put in more time at the school. He wanted to be with J.J., of course, but he also enjoyed Colly's company. Since she'd turned down all offers of dates thus far, it was the only way he could be near her. He read the parenting books she recommended in order to have an excuse to discuss them with her, and surprised himself by enjoying them.

Knowledge gained from the so-called experts gave him confidence. It was comforting to learn that no one was born knowing how to raise children. For some, like Colly, communicating love and acceptance was easy. But parents, after all, were mortal beings and they made mistakes. He was not alone.

Since meeting Colly, he'd relinquished some duties to his employees and taken unheard-of afternoons off. The time he spent with his son was filled with discovery for both of them. They shopped the Christmas-filled malls and came home laden with gifts and decorations and happy memories. They spent hours playing in the snow that had come unusually early for Oklahoma, and more hours warming up with big mugs of Brigit's homemade cocoa.

The tension and pressure in his life lost its power over him as he learned to laugh at the antics of cartoon characters with his giggling son. Surprisingly, he felt little guilt when they "wasted" a whole snowy afternoon working on a jigsaw puzzle. He and J.J. played and talked and took naps curled up in each other's arms. They were making up for lost time and learning how to live with each other.

They were having fun, but whenever he stopped to think about it, as he did now, James realized that underlying the joy was a sense of desperation. Maybe what they were really doing was learning that they couldn't live without each other.

The story ended and Luz ushered the children to the tables for an afternoon snack of muffins and juice. J.J. waved at him as he settled into his little chair. James waved back and added a conspiratorial wink.

"I wasn't expecting you today." Colly grinned as she approached him.

"I had some free time and thought I'd drop by. I hope that's not a problem."

"It's never a problem to have extra hands. Especially when it's too cold to play outside."

"Brigit wanted me to thank you for taking J.J. to the Y for his swimming lesson yesterday."

"How's she feeling? Wisdom teeth can cause a lot of pain." Colly's concern was genuine. In the past few weeks she'd developed a warm relationship with the

Townsends' housekeeper, helping her out with J.J. when she could.

"She needs to have them extracted," he told her. "She's trying to work out a time for the appointment."

"Tell her I'll be happy to keep J.J. after school again. I can take him to his lessons."

"He'd like that. He told me he finally jumped off the diving board. That must have been for your benefit."

"He does seem more willing to take risks now, but I can't claim all the credit. His new security with you and his friendship with David have helped him overcome his shyness."

"You've been good for him, Colly. And for me." James knew her influence was largely responsible for not only the changes in J.J., but those in himself as well. Her acceptance had strengthened the boy's self-esteem and given him the courage to try new things. Her encouragement helped James overcome his self-doubts and reassured him that he could be the father J.J. needed.

He wanted to tell her how much he appreciated the contribution she'd made, but someone's juice spilled and she hurried to the kitchen for a towel.

He followed her to the tiny galley after the mess was cleaned up. Offering him a pumpkin muffin, she said, "You have to try one. The children made them this morning and J.J. put in the raisins."

Colly hoped eating the muffin would keep James occupied for a few minutes. He'd had a look of longing in his eyes when he told her how good she'd been for him and J.J. He obviously had something on his mind and she wasn't sure she was ready to discuss that something just now. She'd spent far more time with the Townsend men than was wise and feared she was becoming too important to them. It was a dead-sure certainty that they had become too important to her.

She dropped the wet towel into the linen hamper and when she turned she was practically in James's arms.

"Colly, will you have dinner with me tonight?" Careful not to touch her, he braced his hands casually on the counter at her sides. It wasn't really an embrace, but the stance allowed him to smell the strawberry scent of her hair and feel the warmth of her body without appearing too aggressive.

"Dinner?" she repeated softly.

"Brigit's agreed to stay with J.J. Something important has come up and I need to discuss it with you."

"Wouldn't you rather come by here after the kids go home?" she asked.

"No, I wouldn't. This isn't about business."

"It isn't?" Colly's heart thumped in her chest. That left only pleasure.

"For once I'd like to be alone with you, Colly. Or at least as alone as we can be in a restaurant full of people. We've known each other for weeks. Don't you trust me enough to have dinner with me?"

His words, spoken in a husky whisper, made her heart race. It was an exciting prospect, but being alone with James probably wasn't a good idea. So far, she'd made it clear that the times they spent together were not dates. But now, as the crisp scent of his after-shave invaded her senses, her reaction to his nearness proved just how futile self-delusion could be.

He strained toward her without moving a muscle and she could almost feel the nubby texture of his suit coat. His lips parted slightly, drawing her glance, and the light shadow of beard along his jaw begged for her touch. If she touched him, she'd want to kiss him. And if she kissed him, she'd want to . . .

No. She couldn't let the memory of other kisses sabotage good sense. Not here and especially not in front of the children. She'd shown remarkable restraint thus far, but it was hard to be objective when his warm lips were only a breath away.

She'd almost summoned the strength to step away from him when she recalled her horoscope for the day. Amazingly, it had said that a major breakthrough could come from a romantic dinner. At the time she hadn't given it a second thought, but now . . .

Who was she to interfere with fate, especially when it gave her permission to do what she wanted to do all along? Before she could talk herself out of it, she blurted, "Would you like to have dinner at my house instead?"

The invitation itself wasn't half as startling as the breathless way in which it was delivered. James smiled at the look of consternation on Colly's face. It was a look that said if he hesitated, she'd renege and send him packing. "I'd love to. Is seven o'clock all right?"

"That's fine," she said, still able to think of little else but kissing him.

"Okay, you two, break it up in here." Luz breezed in with the empty juice cups. "Such behavior is a bad influence."

"On the children?" Embarrassed, Colly ducked away from James and busied herself stacking cups in the dishwasher.

"No, on me. I'm a betrothed woman whose man is out of town."

James stayed until the school day was over, reading to the children and helping with a craft project. As soon as he and J.J. left, Colly began gathering her things.

"You don't mind closing up for me, do you, Luz?"

"What's your hurry, girl? I usually have to pry you out of this place with a crowbar."

"I'm expecting a guest for dinner."

"Anyone I know?" Luz teased, as if she had no idea who'd been romancing Colly in the kitchen.

Colly evaded the question with one of her own. "What can I serve that's easy but tastes like it's not?"

"You want my advice, order a pizza."

"I've cooked for you before, haven't I?" Colly had never taken the time to perfect her culinary skills and couldn't hold the comment against her friend.

Luz nodded and wrinkled her pert nose in mock disgust. "That's why I suggested ordering in."

Colly buttoned up her fifties-style swirl coat. "I can't serve him pizza. It's not special enough."

"I don't think he's coming for the food, girl. The way he was looking at you in the kitchen, you could serve him lint à la mode, and he wouldn't notice."

Colly laughed because she knew it was true. She'd seen that look, too, and it had made her temporarily insane enough to ignore all the warning signals. She'd since had second thoughts about entertaining James at her house, horoscope or no horoscope. With no children around to chaperone, how would she resist a man who had lately become irresistible?

"I think I'll pick up something at the deli."

Luz's laughter followed her out the door. "If what they say about the way to a man's heart being through his stomach is true, I think that would be a very good idea."

Colly showered when she got home and changed into a pair of baggy tweed trousers and a bronze-colored silk shirt with wide shoulder pads. She glanced at the kitchen clock, a black cat whose big eyes and long tail ticked back and forth with each passing second. James was due soon.

Everything was ready. She'd bought lasagna made by her neighborhood deli and it was warming in the oven alongside a loaf of crusty Italian bread. She'd made a salad and put it, and a bottle of Chianti, in the fridge. The deli clerk had talked her into buying chocolate cheesecake for dessert, which she planned to serve with coffee.

The elderly doorbell chirped and she hurried through the little house to answer it. James blew in, along with a chilly gust of wind. His dark hair was tousled and his face was reddened by the cold.

"It's been an amazing winter. Do you think we'll get more snow tonight?" she asked as she hung his overcoat and scarf in the hall closet.

"It feels like it." He wore a richly hued burgundy sweater over a plaid shirt and gray slacks. After smoothing his hair with one hand, he reached in his pocket and withdrew a small, beribboned box.

"What's this?" she asked when he offered it to her.

"It's customary to bring the hostess flowers, but the real thing wouldn't have lasted a minute in this weather."

She opened the box and found a small cloisonné brooch nestled inside. It was obviously old, but the brightly colored nosegay and hand-painted bow hadn't faded with time. It was exactly the kind of piece she would have chosen, and James's perception pleased her.

"It's lovely."

"I don't normally frequent antique shops, but we passed one on the way home this afternoon and something made me stop. I didn't know what I was looking for until I found it. J.J. thought you'd like it."

"I love it," she said as she pinned the brooch to her lapel. "Thank you very much. Now I can have flowers all the time, even in winter."

He'd hoped for a thank-you kiss, but her satisfied comment and sincere expression would have to do. "Something smells good," he said appreciatively.

"It's lasagna, but I have to confess up front that I did not make it. I'm really not much of a cook."

"One of your few shortcomings."

"And significant only to those who like to eat," she said wryly.

"Personally, I think people spend entirely too much time eating. There are many more interesting things to do."

His voice was unconsciously seductive and Colly had a crazy impulse to ask him what he had in mind. No, she didn't need to know, she was already nervous enough. Her gaze locked with his for a lingering moment before she asked him if he wanted to see the house.

What James wanted was to pull her into his arms for a long, uninterrupted kiss. A kiss that could express the longing and need he felt. A kiss that could say the things he was too confused to say. That's what he wanted to do, but what he said was, "Sure."

He knew she was an enthusiastic collector with a fondness for the past. He expected her home to reflect her interest and it did, in spades. The bungalow, itself a relic of the postwar building boom, was decorated with eclectic flair. Its polished wood floors and pristinely white walls provided a crisp backdrop for an amusing juxtaposition of furniture and accessories from bygone eras.

In the living room a velvet Victorian sofa, fresh from Granny's parlor, shared space with pink molded plastic chairs salvaged from a dentist's waiting room. Mirrored shelves on one wall held an extensive collection of pink Depression glass while the ones opposite housed rows of children's metal lunch pails from the sixties and seventies. James recognized some of the more colorful ones since Colly often carried the little boxes instead of handbags.

They walked down a wide hall. The walls were decorated with vintage knit bathing suits from the twenties suspended from weather-beaten canoe paddles. When they came to the spare bedroom she used as a study, she hesitated momentarily before opening the door.

"This is my cozy room, so please excuse the mess."

He promised and stepped inside. The room was indeed cozy, a crazy-quilt jumble of plants and books and baskets of magazines. Chinese paper shades were drawn down to keep out the night, art deco floor lamps turned up for light. Her cluttered desk consisted of a black-lacquered door atop two red metal file cabinets, the drawers barely closing on the avalanche of papers inside.

Framed family photographs crowded the table tops and for seating there was an old-fashioned fainting bench upholstered in an outrageous fake black and white cowhide fabric. Visual interest was supplied by the Woodstock-era psychedelic posters on the walls.

Only in her dreamy cloud of a bedroom had Colly given free rein to her romantic nature. Propriety allowed James only a glimpse of that room, but it was long enough for him to appreciate the charm of the white-on-white decorating scheme.

And to fantasize about making love to Colly in the white-painted iron bed surrounded by her collection of lacy pillows.

Such thoughts were counterproductive and he banished them from his mind. A quick glance revealed a wicker rocker in front of the window and an elaborate silver-backed dresser set atop a wicker trunk at the foot of the bed. What was left of the negotiable space was filled with an unusual collection of old-time leather baby boots and pewter-framed tintypes of infants and children.

They passed through the dining room on their way to the kitchen at the back of the house. Candles burned on the pine trestle table where two places were set with homespun place mats and mismatched earthenware. The centerpiece was a rhinestone-encrusted cowboy hat filled with silk flowers. The silence was broken by a half a dozen Bavarian cuckoo clocks tick-tocking noisily on the wall.

They ended the tour in a kitchen right out of a 1952 sitcom. James half expected Ethel Mertz to pop in to borrow a cup of sugar. The gas range was a three-burner model, the stubby refrigerator had a cooler on top, and the countertops were an incredible shade of pink. A chrome and black dinette set stood in the middle of the room.

"That's it. What do you think?" Colly checked the oven and the aroma of baking cheese and tomato sauce filled the room.

"It's exactly what I expected," he told her.

"Really?" His answer surprised her because when it came to decorating Colly had always indulged her need to do the unexpected.

"Your house is just like you," he clarified. "It's unusual."

"I'll take that as a compliment."

"It was meant as one."

"Actually this is my grandmother's house. When she joined the Peace Corps she let me rent it for a shamelessly small pittance. When she gets back from Zimbabwe, I'll have to find another place to live."

"You have a grandmother in the Peace Corps in Africa?" he asked in amazement.

"Sure. Doesn't everyone?"

"You come from such an unconventional family, I guess it's no surprise that some of your collections are a bit..."

"Weird?" she supplied.

"I was going to say bizarre."

"Thank you. Mom thinks I should pick out one of them and work on making it impressive. But I've always been fickle when it comes to commitment."

"You told me once your interest is easily distracted." James wondered what he'd have to do to hold her attention long enough to get past the friends stage.

"It's true. I like too many things. Take the pictures in the bedroom, for example. Whenever I find an old, dusty, forgotten photograph of a baby, I have to buy it."

"You mean those aren't your ancestors?"

"Heavens, no! But they were somebody's little darlings. It's fun to give them names and invent lives for them."

"You're a born storyteller, but I think you have trouble with reality sometimes. The worlds you create are more genuine to you than the ones that exist."

She considered that statement while she took out the bottle of wine. "I think that's a nice way to call me a dreamer, but I can't argue."

"There's nothing wrong with dreams—"

"So long as they don't get in the way of reality?" she finished for him. "Have a seat and I'll pour the wine. It's the cheap stuff but it's not bad."

James was continually amazed by the way Colly changed subjects to suit herself, with no apparent regard for whether or not the issue was resolved. He went along with her, but knew the day would come when they'd have to finish this conversation.

"I get the feeling everything in your house was chosen for its shock value," he observed as he accepted a goblet of wine.

She took the loaf of bread from the oven and arranged the slices in a napkin-lined basket. "Actually, my decorating motto is simple. If an item doesn't add to my comfort or my pleasure, I don't have time for it."

Setting his wineglass on the table, he stepped up behind her. He'd been thinking about this moment all day. "Do your personal relationships have to meet the same criteria?"

"Of course." She thought to be glib and was surprised at the breathlessness of her words. When James opened his arms to her she stepped into them with a strong sense of inevitability. According to her horoscope, she was on the verge of a major breakthrough. She was determined to give it a chance. Without a word, his lips lowered to hers. His kiss touched her like a whisper, unbearable in its tenderness. There was no urgency in the caress, no demand. The gentle exploration was a purely sensual experience that slowly, one by one, drugged each of her senses. They could afford to let it go on and on because they finally had the house and the night all to themselves.

Colly's sigh of pleasure had a quickening effect on James. His arms tightened around her and his attitude became more serious. His tongue sent currents of desire racing through her and she gave herself to the passion she felt—her own as well as his.

Locked together in the warm, lasagna-scented kitchen, they hungered more for what they could give each other than for the food she'd prepared.

Colly was the first to acknowledge the danger and the first to turn her lips away from his. But she didn't move. She stood quietly in the circle of his arms, her big eyes half-closed, her well-kissed lips tingling with the heat of his desire.

"You look like an earthquake survivor," he teased.

"It wasn't an earthquake, but it was the first time I've ever come close to feeling the earth move."

"Let's hope it isn't the last."

The promise in his eyes made her dizzy. She shook her head as if to clear it and stepped away from him. "If you'll give my senses a minute to recover from the overload, I'll get dinner on the table."

James released her, careful to conceal his grin. He felt a little short-circuited himself, but he wasn't honest enough to admit it. Colly's guilelessness was refreshing. There was no pretense about her, no coy manipulating. A man knew where he stood with her. Her lack of ulterior motives was a big part of her charm.

She was still a bit shaky as she pulled the pan of fragrant pasta from the oven. She retrieved the salad from the refrigerator and handed him the bowl to carry into the dining room.

They shared conversation and wine as they ate, talking for nearly two hours about the things that mattered to them. Normally, James wasn't much of a talker and his self-disclosures surprised him. Colly had a knack for making him feel comfortable.

Finally, they returned their dishes to the kitchen and took their coffee and dessert to the living room. Colly had waited all evening for James to discuss the important matter he'd mentioned, but her patience had not paid off.

She could wait no longer and as she settled on the sofa beside him she prompted, "You had something important to talk about."

"I did?"

"That's what you said when you wangled an invitation to dinner."

"As I recall, there was very little wangling involved." She frowned at him and he pretended to recall. "Oh, that. I just wanted to tell you the deal went through on the house today."

"What house?" Colly was confused. In his business, deals went through on houses every day.

"The one you thought I couldn't live without. The one with the broken windows and sagging staircase and peeling paint."

Understanding finally dawned. "The Victorian? Oh, James, that's wonderful." She punched him playfully on the arm. "Why didn't you say something before?"

"I wanted to wait until the owners accepted my offer."

"I'm so happy for you. When will you start the renovations?"

"As soon as I can locate a contractor. Maybe your father could give me some names."

"I'm sure he can, he's had a lot of experience dealing with remodeling."

"I've never done anything like this, so I'll need all the advice I can get."

"You sound worried."

"I am. This is a major undertaking."

She agreed. It was also a major commitment. Buying the house was a sign that James was thinking about the future. Maybe he'd been listening to her after all. "J.J. must be thrilled."

"I haven't told him yet. I wanted you to be the first to know. It's because of you that I'm embarking on this nightmare project." There was more truth in his words than his bantering tone revealed. From the moment he'd kissed Colly on the veranda, James had known that the house was meant for them.

"It won't be a nightmare, everything will work out fine. You made the right decision."

He shook his head. "I'll know that after I get the contractor's estimate. I may be biting off more than I can handle. I don't know much about restoration projects."

"I do," she told him. "I'll be glad to help. I can give you the names of companies that sell authentic Victorian millwork and reproduction antique hardware. When you're ready to furnish, I can show you every hole-in-the-wall antique shop in a three-county area."

Colly's enthusiasm was contagious and before long they had discussed both short-term and long-range plans for the house. When the coffee ran out, James realized how late it had become.

"I should be going," he said.

"Yes, you should."

"It's cold out there."

"And warm in here," she pointed out unnecessarily.

"The thing is, I don't want to leave."

"I don't want you to."

"But I can't stay all night."

"No, you can't do that."

His grin was rakish. "I could stay part of the night."

She concealed her own smile. "I don't think that would be wise."

"No," he agreed. "It would probably be very unwise." He reached for her but she stood up and moved toward the front door. James followed closely.

"I can't let you kiss me like that again, James. If you do, I won't be responsible for my actions."

"I like irresponsible women," he told her.

"Let's think about it. About what we want."

"That's the problem. I know exactly what I want."

She took his coat from the closet and urged him into it. "So do I. It's the same thing I want and if we don't stop wanting it, we're going to get ourselves into trouble."

He didn't like it, but he had to agree with her. "You're a very sensible lady."

"It's a dirty job but somebody has to do it."

"So you're saying we should cool it?" At her nod he shrugged in a hopeless, I-tried gesture.

"I'm glad you understand, James."

"But I don't."

"Then I'm glad you didn't ask me to explain."

"Let me ask you something else. Will you spend Christmas Eve with me and J.J.?"

She hadn't been expecting that and took a moment to consider the invitation. Christmas Eve was a special holiday and spending it together might have serious implications. Things were very close to getting out of hand where James was concerned and she knew she shouldn't spend any more time with him than was necessary to promote her goals.

On the other hand, she wanted to urge him to seek permanent custody of J.J. and Christmas Eve would be a perfect opportunity to do so. She accepted his invitation, but felt a moment of guilt that her motives were a little less than honest.

They agreed to make definite plans later and she reached for the doorknob. He stopped her. "Are you really going to send me out into the freezing night?"

"I really am." She draped his woolen scarf around his neck and made a big show of knotting it securely.

"At least give me a kiss to warm me up before I leave."

She sighed in exasperation and bestowed a formal peck on his forehead. "There. That should hold you until you get your heater revved up."

"My heater's already revved up, but thanks for the thought," he teased.

"You're welcome. Good night, James."

"Good night, Colly." He stepped out onto the icy porch. "You really think we should cool it?"

"I really do."

"That won't be too difficult in this weather," he grumbled. "It's damn cold out here."

"You'd better hurry then." She blew him another kiss and pulled the glass storm door shut behind him. She smiled as he made his way down the slippery walk and watched until his car pulled away from the curb.

She locked the door and went into the living room to clear away the coffee cups. For a moment there, her resolve had weakened and she'd been tempted to call him back into the warm house and into her arms. The thought of spending the whole long night with James was enough to sabotage even a sensible lady's good intentions.

Chapter Seven

A week before Christmas, Colly invited James to a showing of her parents' work and to the reception that followed. The Flower Child Gallery was located on historic Paseo Street, a three block stretch of Spanish mission revival architecture originally built in 1929. The Paseo was lined with art galleries, ethnic restaurants and import shops. It was peopled with artists, tourists and resident bohemians.

It was Saturday so James picked Colly up at home and they drove to the gallery together. It was another almost-but-not-quite-date date.

Peter and Pamela Fairchild welcomed the couple and personally showed James around the studio and gallery, which was housed in a renovated warehouse and occupied two barnlike floors. Though cold, the day was clear. Hard-edged sunlight streamed through the banks of windows, showing off the exhibits of stained glass to advantage.

The Fairchilds' art ranged in size from full-scale windows to tiny, jewel-toned sun catchers. They worked on many projects together, but each had a special area of interest. Peter's collection of lamp shades, designed in the Tiffany tradition, generated excitement among the gallery visitors. Pamela's specialty was delicate boxes, which were every bit as exquisite as the jewelry they were designed to hold. James bought one in his mother's favorite colors for a Christmas gift.

He wandered around while Colly mingled with the guests. She rejoined him a few minutes later and took his arm. "I want to show you my all-time favorite piece of my parents' work."

She led him to an alcove at the back of the gallery in which a large triptych titled Enchantment was displayed. Track lights bathed it in artificial sunshine and intensified the colors, which glowed with inner fire. The three-foot-tall center panel depicted a fairy-tale vision of a medieval castle, its turrets and towers entwined with vines and windswept roses.

In the left panel, a silvery white unicorn stood watch in an emerald forest. Rendered in cold hard glass, the creature took on amazing life in the hands of artists as skilled as the Fairchilds. The detail was incredible, from the tiny flowers in the flowing mane to the flashing platinum hooves and gleaming horn.

The right panel portrayed a knight in armor embracing a lady with billowing yellow hair. His faithful steed, in full battle regalia, waited patiently nearby. Created in the true spirit of romance, the scene evoked the mysticism of the age of chivalry. James, who was not easily enchanted, admired the piece and could understand Colly's affection for it.

"I'm impressed," he said sincerely. "Until today, I thought stained glass was just for church windows."

She smiled. "If you could make a poem out of glass, this would be it. I think it's the most beautiful thing my parents ever made."

"Not counting you, my dear." Her father joined them in time to hear Colly's remark. She turned up her cheek in a teasing bid for a kiss and James felt the warmth shared by father and daughter.

"The show's a success, isn't it?" she asked her father.

"I'd say so." The tall man looked more leonine than ever with his flowing hair and fashionably baggy black suit. Turning to James, he asked, "Were any of those contractors whose names I gave you able to help?"

"Yes, thanks again. I accepted a bid from Singer and Sons. They've already begun work. If you have time, I'd like to talk to you about replacing a fanlight and some windows in the house."

"I always have time for potential customers," Peter said with a grin that was very much like Colly's. "Let's go in my workroom where it's quieter. You can tell me what you have in mind."

The two excused themselves and Colly watched them walk away. They were both strikingly handsome men and it amused her to see women's heads turn as they passed.

"I like your young man," Colly's mother whispered as she walked up behind her.

"I like yours, too," Colly quipped.

"James rather surprises me, though," Pamela admitted.

"In what way?"

"He's so serious. You've never been interested in serious men before."

"I've never been serious about a man before."

"And you are this time?"

"I don't know. When I'm not with him, I feel like I'm just marking time. When I am with him, I have trouble breathing and talking at the same time. It's all very confusing."

Pamela patted her daughter's shoulder in a comforting gesture. "Love is confusing most of the time, dear."

Colly looked alarmed. "Oh, no, I don't think I'm falling in love."

"All the symptoms are there. Would it be so terrible if you were?"

"It would be disastrous." She'd always been able to talk to her mother about everything and this was no exception. She explained how she'd contrived to further her cause and bring James and J.J. closer together. And how in doing so, she had inadvertently carved out a niche for herself in their lives.

"Connived would be more like it," her mother said grimly.

"I had the best of intentions," Colly defended.

"Columbine Ariel Fairchild! How many times have I warned you not to interfere in people's lives?"

"Is that a trick question?"

Pamela shook her head. "I knew your meddling would backfire on you someday. Now James is in love with you."

"Surely not. I think he's probably just grateful for the help I've given him. That's all."

"It's not gratitude I see in his eyes when he looks at you, Colly," Pamela said softly.

"Really?"

"Really. Honey, I know you're young, but I can't believe you didn't recognize love when it fell in your lap."

"Maybe you're wrong." Colly wasn't ready for real love. She wasn't equipped to handle the emotional stress such a responsibility would bring. Love and commitment were such grown-up ideas, and in many ways Colly didn't consider herself a grown-up yet.

"For everyone's sake, I hope I am."

"What am I going to do if you're right?"

"I don't know. But whatever you do, be careful. You're dealing with a very fragile commodity here—the happiness of another person. I'd hate to see James get hurt. And J.J."

"J.J.?"

"The child adores you, Colly. Surely you realize that?"

"At the risk of sounding immodest, all my students adore me."

"Your other students aren't looking for a substitute mother. Tread gently when you're walking on hearts, dear."

Colly sighed. "I care about James and J.J., but how can I know if what I feel is love? The real kind that lasts forever?"

"How does anyone ever know?"

"You and Dad knew when you were younger than I am now," she reminded her mother.

"When something is right, be it love or anything else, your heart will tell you."

"And I'll know? Just like that?"

"You'll know."

Her mother's words sounded wise, but were too cryptic to offer Colly much comfort.

On Christmas Eve Colly drove to the big Victorian house only two blocks from her parents' home. James's choice of location for the celebration had surprised her, but she hadn't questioned his decision. Parking her van at the curb, she smiled at the decorations. Someone had been very busy since she'd last dropped by.

Evergreen boughs and miniature white lights twined around the porch pillars and swagged from the railings, adding a festive air to the empty house. The upstairs windows were dark, but welcoming light blazed from the windows on the ground floor.

Clutching her bag of gifts, she made her way up the walk and lifted the heavy brass knocker. It had recently been polished. J.J., decked out in a green velvet blazer and red bow tie, answered the door.

"Colly!"

"J.J.!" Their customary greeting never failed to make them laugh. "How handsome you look."

"Brigit got me the bow tie," he explained as he fidgeted with the neck gear. "Is it dorky?"

"I think it's very festive."

"I thought it was dorky, but I didn't want to hurt Brigit's feelin's."

"That was very sensitive of you."

Her comment seemed to please him. "We've been waitin' for you. Dad said we couldn't open any presents or eat any goodies till you got here."

Colly stepped into the foyer, which was lit by a bare bulb in the ceiling. Painters' drop cloths were draped over the banisters and shoved into corners. Paint cans and equipment had been temporarily abandoned. Someone had attempted to sweep up the sawdust and loose plaster, but it was pervasive and had settled on everything.

Taking her hand, J.J. led Colly into the living room. The first thing she noticed was the enormous Christmas tree, decorated like a dream and surrounded by brightly wrapped packages. The second thing she noticed was James.

He was kneeling in front of the huge fireplace, feeding an already roaring fire. He stood up when he saw her and dusted his hands on his trousers.

"Come in and try to make yourself at home." He looked around apologetically at the mess the workmen had left. "It probably seems crazy to invite you to this cold, empty house when there's a perfectly good furnished condo across town."

"It's not so cold," she said with a glance at the fireplace. "Or so empty." Her smile said the company more than made up for the lack of furnishings.

"You don't think it's silly that J.J. and I wanted to celebrate Christmas in our new house?"

"You shouldn't have spent it anywhere else."

"How do you like the tree, Colly?" J.J. chirped.

"It's a vision." The artificial fir sparkled with lights and tinsel and garlands of pearls. It was laden with wispy-haired angels, silver balls and crystal icicles.

"Me and Dad saw it at the Christmas store in the mall," J.J. told her. "He told the lady he'd take it and everything on it. They just delivered it this afternoon. It took a whole bunch of guys and a big truck. Wow, was that somethin'. One minute there was no tree and then poof! there it was."

"That's what Christmas is all about, right?" James asked. "Magic."

J.J. pulled Colly down on a quilt spread on the floor. Nearby were silver trays containing plates of canapés and a carafe of eggnog. "We're having a picnic. I said you can't have a picnic in the winter, but Dad said sure we could. So we are." His thin shoulders bobbed in an eloquent shrug and Colly found it hard to believe that this bubbly child was the same withdrawn little kid she'd first seen at Shady Dell three months ago.

That day he'd stood in the doorway, unsure whether to run away or cry. It had taken a solid week of patient coaxing to get even a few words out of him.

She reminded herself that at the time J.J.'s mother had recently abandoned him. The poor little guy didn't know if his father would be there for him or not and wasn't sure if there was a grown-up alive that he could trust. He'd come a long way since then, she decided as she watched him snuggle into James's lap. Happiness and contentment were etched in their matching smiles.

They were so perfect together, father and son. Maybe they would have found their way to each other without her help. Maybe. But there was a big possibility that they never would have. She could be proud of what she'd done, even if it was, in her mother's words, meddling. No matter how things turned out for her and James, she would have no regrets.

"Now that Colly's here, can we eat?" J.J. looked into James's face. "I'm getting pretty hungry."

"Help yourself, champ."

He scampered over to the hors d'oeuvres tray and James scooted across the quilt to sit beside Colly. "I'm glad you could come. I'll have to thank your family for sharing you with us tonight."

"They've all gone to a party at their friends' house. We'll be getting together tomorrow. You and J.J. are welcome to join us."

"No," he declined. "That's for family."

She wanted to tell him that he and J.J. were like part of the family, but knew the words would sound trite. She'd also feel like a hypocrite saying them when she wasn't willing to open herself up to that possibility.

James surprised her when he added, "J.J. and I are going to Dallas in the morning to spend a few days with my mother and stepfather."

"I'm glad to hear that, James."

"Yeah, I figured it was about time. Mother hasn't had a chance to spend much time with J.J. and I think he should get to know his grandmother."

"So do I." Colly had never pried too deeply into James's relationship with his mother, but she knew they had never been close. His new attitude toward his family was reassuring.

"Yuck." J.J. was eyeing the food tray with skepticism. "What're these brown things on the cheese and crackers?"

"Smoked oysters," James informed him.

"Do I like 'em?"

"I don't know. Try one and see."

"They look gross," he insisted.

"But they taste delicious." Colly encouraged him by leaning over and popping one in her mouth.

J.J.'s expression said that he found her look of ecstasy somewhat contrived. "I'll try one but if I don't like it, can I spit it out?"

James handed him a napkin for that purpose, but J.J. didn't use it. "They're not too bad. But I like the teeny weenies better."

James brought Colly up to date on the renovations. According to the general contractor, the floors were in excellent shape and only required sanding and refinishing. The plumbing contractor had pronounced the old copper pipes adequate and had ordered new fixtures for the bathrooms and kitchen. The heat and air man was installing a new furnace and central air-conditioning unit. Living in an authentically preserved home was one thing, doing without air-conditioning in Oklahoma's muggy summer weather was quite another.

A crew had begun the onerous task of scraping eighty years worth of paint and wallpaper off the walls and that accounted in large part for the dust.

"Did the contractor give you a move-in date?" she asked.

"If nothing unforeseen occurs—and I understand that's a big if in this business—three months."

"Can we open the presents now?" J.J. had finished eating and his attention had once again focused on the packages under the tree.

James shook his head and before J.J. could complain, the strains of "We Wish You a Merry Christmas" came from outside. They all got up and hurried to the front door. A group of carolers stood at the bottom of the steps, filling the night with the sounds of Christmas.

The singers, many of whom Colly knew from the neighborhood, invited them to join them on their rounds. The night was cold and still. A bright moon shone down on the thin layer of snow, making it sparkle like the glitter snow on a Christmas card. Bundled into warm coats, Colly and James snuggled J.J. between them and held hands as they sang the old familiar carols.

They returned home an hour later, cold and filled with the spirit of Christmas.

"You know," James said as he stashed their coats, "that's the first time I've ever been caroling."

"You're kidding." Colly couldn't believe his life had been so deprived.

He seemed amazed himself. "To tell the truth, I never would have taken the time for such a thing. It really was nice." The nicest part, he didn't add, was holding hands with Colly and pretending that the three of them were a family.

"Now can we open the presents?" J.J. prodded.

James looked at Colly and together they chorused, "Now!"

J.J. wasted no time tearing into his gifts, which turned out to be an assortment of clothing and toys he'd asked for. He oohed and ahed over each one for only a moment before heading for the next package.

Colly opened her present from J.J. and found a clumsily made little Christmas tree ornament that she would treasure always. Also in the package were a pair of dainty silver earrings.

"I got you two gifts," J.J. explained, "'Cause you can only use the decoration at Christmas. The earrings you can wear all the time."

"And I shall," she assured him.

Colly's gifts to James were an imported Fair Isle sweater and one of her parents' sun catchers in the shape of a soaring kite. He held it up and it caught the light from the tree, reminding them both of their own kite flying experience and the kisses they'd shared that windswept autumn day.

James handed Colly a large box wrapped in silver paper and tied with a big red bow. She opened it and removed its contents from the tissue paper nest.

"James! This is beautiful." She stood up and held the dress against her. The vintage Victorian gown had faded from its original white to a subtle cream color. It had a tall, stand-up collar edged in lace and leg-of-mutton sleeves. Panels of lace were set into the gored skirt and the back closed with tiny pearl buttons.

"I hope it fits," he told her. "The lady at the shop said you could return it if it didn't."

"I'll make it fit," she said. "I wouldn't dream of returning anything as beautiful as this."

"It looks like a bride dress," J.J. put in.

"It might have been, but probably some lady had it made to wear to parties and other special occasions," she explained.

Colly wanted to say more about the thoughtfulness of the gift, but J.J. began unwrapping her present to him—a big, floppy teddy bear in a herringbone vest and deerstalker hat.

"His name is Archibald," Colly told him seriously. "And he's a very adventurous bear."

James slipped out of the room while Colly was telling J.J. the story of how Archibald had called out to her in a toy store and asked her if she knew any little boys who needed a special friend. He came back a minute later with a large box. The air holes punched in the sides were a dead giveaway as to its contents, but J.J. was so enraptured with the story of Archibald, he didn't seem to notice.

James waited until the story was finished. "J.J., I found one more present for you and it's a big one."

J.J. ripped off the ribbon and flung open the lid of the box. He peeked in and looked up a second later with a look of wonder on his face. "There's something in there."

"Like what?" James asked innocently.

"Something warm and furry. It licked me." Just then the box tumbled over and a fat golden ball of fur rolled out. "It's a puppy! A real live puppy!"

Colly couldn't decide which of the Townsends looked happiest, J.J. for receiving such a gift, or James for giving it.

"Is he mine?"

"The box had your name on it," his father told him.
"That means he'll be your responsibility. You have to
feed him and water him and clean up after him."

"And love him," Colly put in. "That's very important, too."

"I will. I mean I do. I already love him. What's his
name?"

James was still beaming. "You have to give him one."

"It has to be something special," J.J. said solemnly.
"'Cause he's a special dog. Lemme think about it."

J.J. and the little golden retriever romped away. All of
his other gifts, including Archibald the bear, were temporarily forgotten. Not even an adventuring teddy could
compete with a real live puppy.

When the dog wandered too far, J.J. delighted in calling him back. The two were quickly becoming insepara-
ble.

"That was a very nice thing you did," Colly told
James. "Those two are going to have a lot of fun growing up together."

"A boy should have a dog. And now that we have the
house, there's plenty of room."

This was just the opening she'd wanted. "Does that
mean J.J. will be staying with you for good?"

"I don't know. I talked to Lenore the other day and
she's coming back to the States in a couple of months."

Colly's stomach tightened. "How do you feel about
that?"

"Confused. She met some guy in Europe. He's from
Los Angeles and she's moving out there."

"Does she want to take J.J. with her?"

"She says she's not sure it would be the best environ-
ment for him. She's willing to discuss giving me custody."

Colly had felt a moment of dread when James first mentioned his ex-wife. All she felt now was relief. "That's wonderful."

"I know." His words, his tone of voice, even his posture said he knew no such thing.

"Aren't you happy?"

"Yeah, I'm happy."

"Excuse me for saying so, but you don't sound happy. What's wrong, James?"

"I just don't know what to do. Lenore loves J.J. as much as I do. She was crying and carrying on something awful on the phone."

"She hasn't been a very big part of his life," Colly pointed out.

"You can't criticize her without criticizing me. All in all, she's spent more time with him than I have."

"But you're trying to make up for that."

"I'm trying, but how do I know if I can ever really make up for leaving him when he was a baby? And if I take his mother's love away from him, he might grow to resent me."

"Surely she'd want visitation."

"I'm sure she would. And J.J. would be torn between us. I can't do that to him."

Colly decided to try another line of attack. "J.J. idolizes you."

"Yeah, now he does. But taking care of a five-year-old's needs aren't that hard. How will I do when he's ten or fifteen or twenty? When he gets old enough to realize I'm not the super-great guy he thinks I am?"

"You are a super-great guy," she said sincerely. "I've known it all along."

"Hey, J.J.," he called to his romping son. "Don't let the puppy get in the kitchen. There's paint and bad stuff in there."

"Don't worry, Dad," he answered. "I'm taking good care of him, just like you take care of me."

Colly smiled. "See? Even J.J. knows you're doing a good job."

"Thanks for the vote of confidence." He massaged the bridge of his nose in a tired gesture. "God, I love that kid. I can't imagine living without him."

"So what's the problem?"

"I could make all kinds of psychological defenses, but the simple truth is, I'm afraid of messing up. I'm afraid I won't know when to hold on and when to let go. When to give in and when to give up. I remember what you said about a parent giving his children roots and wings. I don't know if I can do that."

"I think you can."

"Maybe his mother would do a better job."

She couldn't let him get into that line of thought. "J.J. needs a father."

"He also needs a mother. I've learned a lot in the past three months, but I'm not so impressed by my progress that I think I can do the job of two parents."

"Lenore can't do the job of two parents, either."

"She's talking about marrying this guy in L.A. My main complaint about her has been her instability. If she's married and settled down things might be better. Who knows? Maybe a mother and a stepfather would be better for J.J. than a father alone."

"I can't believe you think that."

"I don't know what to think," he confessed. "My head tells me one thing and my heart tells me something else."

Colly thought how ironic it was that she'd had a similar conversation with her mother only a week ago. The stakes were different, but the feelings were remarkably the same.

"You and J.J. belong together. You need each other more than any two people I know."

He wanted to ask her where she fit into the picture. Didn't she realize he also needed her? He wasn't brave enough to ask her right out, but unconsciously he'd just made a plea for her to marry him and be J.J.'s mother. He hadn't planned it that way, but that's how it had happened.

And she hadn't gotten the message. She was so young, she probably couldn't imagine dealing with the kinds of problems marriage could bring. Especially marriage to a man with a whole changeable wardrobe of problems of his own.

Colly watched James's struggle and wished there was something she could say or do to help him make his decision. She recalled the advice her mother had given her. "Listen to your heart, James. When a thing is right, your heart will know."

James looked at her and was filled with a rush of emotion that made him reach out to grasp her hand. She was so sincere, so sweet and untouched by life. She had no experience dealing with pain and awful truths. As well-meaning as she was, Colly had no idea what traitors hearts could be.

Chapter Eight

A month later, on the morning of Colly's birthday, the phone rang. She quickly snatched it up, hoping it was James.

It was. "Happy birthday."

Colly was flattered that James remembered. She'd only mentioned the date in passing during their discussion of birthday wishes, back in October. "Thank you."

"I'm sorry I have to be out of town. I would have liked to make your birthday as special as you helped make J.J.'s." He'd only been gone three days and already he was impatient to get home. He hadn't expected to miss her as much as he did.

"The fact that you called is special enough," she said sincerely. They'd spent so much time together since Christmas, she'd thought it was a good thing his business trip to Dallas had come up. She'd hoped to use the separation to restore some objectivity to the relationship. Her plan had backfired, however, and she'd discovered new meaning in the old cliché about absence making the heart grow fonder.

"I talked to J.J. last night," he told her. "He was disappointed that I wouldn't be there to help you celebrate. But he promised to save me a piece of the cake he helped make for you."

"He's such a thoughtful child. It must be an inherited trait." Colly could think of lots of ways to celebrate with James and none of them had anything to do with cake.

"I'll be thinking about you all day and I hope you'll be thinking of me, too."

She thought of little else these days. "I may be too busy celebrating, but I'll try to spare you a few moments."

James laughed and told her that was good enough for him. He promised to see her at the end of the week.

As far as Colly could tell, the biggest advantage of having her birthday on a weekday was that she would be so busy she wouldn't have time to notice how lonely it would be without James.

At school, she and the children cut fat snowmen and fragile snowflakes from white construction paper and decorated the bulletin board. They had just finished when Luz came out of the office.

She clapped her hands together for attention. "Okay, everyone, it's time for the surprise."

The children raced to their cubbies, rifled through their belongings and presented Colly with handmade birthday cards.

"Thank you, class," she said brightly as she collected her bounty and hugged each child in turn. "What a wonderful surprise."

Someone banged on the door and Luz hurried to open it. She came back carrying the biggest bouquet of balloons Colly had ever seen. Some of them had stuffed animals and rag dolls inside. "Luz, did you—"

"You know I don't make that kind of money, girl." Luz grinned and stepped aside. "Maybe you'd better ask Buttons the clown who they're from."

Buttons, who obviously got his name from the dinner-plate sized fasteners on his costume, dropped his large satchel on the floor and bowed with mock dignity. He took the balloons from Luz and passed them to Colly. The children giggled with delight when he gave her a noisy smack on the cheek.

"Okay kids, it's show time. Everybody sing real loud now." He and the children serenaded her with the birthday song, then Buttons directed her to a seat of honor while he entertained them. As he performed magic tricks and made balloon animals for the children, Colly opened the card attached to her bouquet.

Happy birthday, dear Colly. I could have sent flowers and candy or an expensive gift, but I decided that's exactly what you'd expect from me. I wanted to prove to you that Taureans sometimes get a bad rap about having their feet so firmly planted in terra firma. If a cow can jump over the moon, so can Taurus the bull. Anyway, have a great birthday. Love, James.

Colly swallowed the emotional lump in her throat and slipped the card into her pocket. If she kept seeing James, she was going to be sorry. He and J.J. were becoming much too important to her. When he came back she would slowly begin to extricate herself from their daily lives. It was past time to put an end to this madness. It might be a little late, but it was one New Year's resolution she intended to keep.

It was an uncommonly snowy winter, but the weeks wore on and the last snowmen finally melted away. Colly never did get around to keeping the resolution she'd made on her birthday. She kept telling herself that she would start someday. Someday never quite arrived. It was impossible to stay completely away from James.

Spring fever spread unchecked through the Shady Dell Preschool, infecting children and teachers alike. Inside, sentimental Valentine hearts gave up their places on the bulletin board and the shamrocks and kites of March took over. Outside, every new-bloomed daffodil made a promise of spring.

The change of seasons brought renewal to James's life, as well. He'd grown comfortable with his new role as dedicated father and turned his attention to being a better son. He started calling his mother and taking time to send her cards. His efforts were rewarded with an outpouring of love that had been there all along, if only he'd taken time to notice.

After the rush of the holidays was over, he returned to running his business. Overseeing renovations on the house became a full-time job and he and Colly were mostly limited to "school time" and "house time."

A few weekend antiquing excursions netted furnishings and accessories. They gave the obliging owner of one of Colly's favorite shops a list of additional items Colly thought James would need for the house. For a small fee, the woman promised to procure them from other dealers and store them until needed.

If her own busy schedule allowed, Colly accompanied James on his shopping trips. Sometimes, if James was lucky and the moon was just right, she'd drop by the house in the evenings, offering encouragement and insight on everything from the choice of color for the porch pillars to the selection of wallpaper.

Dodging carpenters and painters, he would lure her into a dusty corner where she allowed him to steal a kiss or two, but rarely did they have a chance to be alone. It seemed to him that she planned it that way.

J.J. was happier than ever and took endless pleasure in helping his dad around the new house. James bought him a small tool belt complete with tiny hammer, pliers and an intriguing assortment of wrenches. He soon developed limited skill in their use and gloried in pounding nails in the wood scraps given to him by the workmen.

Colly was secretly grateful for the circumstances that allowed her to put an emotional distance between herself and the Townsends. Her mother's comments about love had shaken her considerably and she'd spent many sleepless nights worrying about that subject. She'd deliberately set out to bring James and J.J. together, but not once had she planned to fall in love. Now that she was frighteningly close to doing so, she didn't quite know how to deal with the situation.

She'd taken on many causes in the past, both personal and civic. She'd felt just as strongly about them as she did this one. But she'd always managed to summon the detachment necessary to move on when her goals were accomplished. Despite her mother's misguided comments and the warnings of her own confused heart, she stubbornly refused to believe that things might be different this time.

Luz accused her of burying her head, ostrich-style, and ignoring the issue, but Colly went blithely on with the business of life. Her philosophical stance was of the tree-falling-in-the-forest variety. A problem couldn't exist unless you acknowledged its existence.

She wasn't ready for a lifelong commitment. She was too young and too unsure about what she wanted from life. She was a free spirit; she couldn't settle down with a ready-made family. She was happy with things the way they were and didn't know if she was willing to change her life to accommodate others. And as her mother had so aptly put it, she wouldn't know love if it dropped in her lap.

All very good reasons, she told herself, not to let her feelings get the best of her. Besides, her internal debate continued, James hadn't said a word about love in all the months she'd known him. So far he hadn't pressed for more than kisses, and he'd given no verbal indication that he wanted more from her than friendship.

She could be a good friend. It was being someone's significant other that she was unsure about.

He hadn't mentioned the custody question since Christmas and she assumed he was still struggling with his conscience. She longed to talk some sense into him, but for once she kept her opinions to herself.

Her overall horoscope for January had been nothing short of cautionary. "The project you've been working on for several months is reaching culmination, but if you push too hard now, all your efforts could be for naught."

February's had told her: "If you are willing to accept a lot of uncertainty, you will set yourself up for some exciting new developments."

Then, when she thought she could take no more tension, her March forecast had warned: "A situation that has not lived up to your expectations may soon resolve itself. It can be transformed into everything you want it to be, but only if you show uncharacteristic patience.''

The stars were trying to tell her something. She'd done all she could do. It was up to James now. Her ''mission'' was almost complete and regardless of his decision, she would soon have no reason to play an active role in their lives. All the more reason to allow things to continue to cool down between them.

One day in early April, James picked up J.J. after school and stayed to talk to Colly. When the last of her charges left, she approached them in the play area.

''Thanks for volunteering to put away the blocks, J.J.,'' she told the boy. ''That's a big help to me.''

James patted his son on the shoulder. ''You keep on working, I want to talk to Colly for a minute.''

''Okay, Dad.'' J.J. bent back to his task, setting the polished wooden blocks in neat rows.

''Guess what?'' James asked as they walked to her little cubicle of an office. ''The last of the workmen left today. The house is finally pronounced finished.''

''That's wonderful. When do you move in?''

''Your friend at the antique shop said she could have my stuff delivered tomorrow. Since I don't know anything about design, I hired a decorator to come in and help me put it all together.''

Colly had hoped that might be her job, but obviously James had other ideas. She silently scolded herself for feeling shut out at the big moment. Wasn't this what she'd been working toward?

''Sounds like you have everything under control,'' she said brightly. ''I can't wait to see it.''

"Which brings me to my next question. I want to have a housewarming party a week from Saturday. Will you come?"

"Of course." Now why had she agreed? She should have begged off if she was really serious about that resolution.

"I'm inviting some people from the office and a few business associates. I'd like to have your parents if you think they'd be interested."

"I'm sure they will be. Do you need any help planning the party?" She could have bitten her tongue. The point was to help them get along without her.

"Nope. It's all taken care of. I'll be so busy moving and settling in, I won't have time to worry about cheese puffs and pâté. I've already hired a caterer to come in and do the party."

"Great." If everything was great, why did she feel so left out?

James thought he saw a flicker of disappointment in Colly's eyes but surely he was mistaken. After all, she was the one who'd had reservations about their relationship. The shoulder she'd given him these past weeks hadn't been exactly cold, but it had definitely been cool. As cool as she'd insisted they keep things between them.

He'd invited her out to dinner several times, but she was always too busy. The demands on his own time were such that he'd finally stopped asking and contented himself with whatever stolen moments she allowed. Their kisses, which had started out so passionate and mind-rattling, had gradually evolved backward into little more than formal Hollywood-style pecks.

Colly wouldn't let him get close and she wouldn't give him a chance to discuss anything that even remotely resembled the future. She'd erected an effective emotional force field around herself that repelled his most ardent advances.

Eventually he'd given up because, as much as he cared for her, there was nothing he could do to change the problems between them. He would always be seven years, and worlds of experience, older. She would always want a carefree, simple life, while his was complicated with problems she had no way of dealing with. He'd always need the security of commitment, while she would, at least until she matured into acceptance, always shy away from making one.

When he thought about it in those terms, James realized all over again how little he and Colly had in common. He only wished he didn't care so much.

"Dad, I'm all done with the blocks," J.J. called.

James and Colly walked to the playroom. "You did an excellent job," she told the child. "Thank you again."

"No problem," he said in a very grown-up voice. "Are you guys through talkin' now? I want to play with Harley." He'd named the puppy after a favorite construction worker who'd given him his first carpentry lessons.

"Sure, son. Get your things and we'll go home."

"To our old home or our new home?"

"Why don't we take a load of your stuff over to our new house tonight and see how it fits in?"

"Yeah! Colly, you gotta see my room. It's really neat, it has giant big ceilings and what do you call those windows?"

"Dormers," James supplied.

"Yeah, dormers. I got to pick out the wallpaper and it has sailboats on it."

"I can't wait to see it," Colly told him. "I could come over and help tonight."

James felt he'd imposed on her too much already. He was worried that she might think he had taken advantage of her generosity. In truth, he had. From now on, he vowed to himself, when they saw each other it would be on a purely social basis.

"I'd really rather you waited until the party when it's all finished," James said hesitantly. "It's just an empty house now. By Saturday night you can get the full effect of the furnishings." And the other surprises he had in store for her.

"Okay, Saturday it is." She shouldn't feel the way she did. It was right that a guest should have to wait until the official unveiling like all the other people he'd invited.

Never mind that she'd been in on the project from the very beginning. If it hadn't been for her James never would have looked twice at the house. He might have needed her help at one time, but now he had control of his life and her services were no longer required. She understood just fine.

Colly knew she was being perverse and it wasn't like her to feel sorry for herself. Things were working out just as she'd planned, so what was her problem? She got herself under control and walked them to the door. She waved as they got in the car.

Father and son were talking and laughing, as happy as she'd ever seen them. Surely James wasn't still considering allowing J.J. to go to California with his mother. She'd longed to ask how that situation was developing, but had to give him the time and space he needed to make his decision. After all, it would affect him and J.J. the rest of their lives and should not be made lightly. And it was really none of her business.

Even if J.J. stayed in Oklahoma City, he'd be going to public kindergarten next year and she'd no longer have an excuse to see him every day. Before long, Shady Dell Preschool and Miss Colly would be a half-forgotten childhood memory. This stupid uncertainty she felt where men were concerned had made her let James slip away. Now she would lose J.J., as well.

Luz had been in the kitchen, washing dishes and staying out of the way. She joined Colly in the doorway and watched the Mercedes drive off.

"Letting go is hard, *amiga*."

"It hurts, too."

"For a while there I thought something good was going to happen between you and Mr. Dream Boat."

"Yeah. For a while..."

"Are you sad about the outcome?"

"I don't really know. You and Mom warned me about meddling in other people's lives. I tried to be objective but it all kind of got away from me."

Luz squeezed her friend's shoulder sympathetically. "Poor Colly. You were so busy trying not to get involved, you didn't notice you were falling in love."

On the afternoon of the party, Colly parked her van at the curb and marveled at the changes in the property. She'd driven by frequently, since her parents lived a few blocks away, but as James said, there was nothing like getting the full effect.

The house had been freshly painted, top to bottom, the clapboards a warm colonial blue, the shutters and trim crisp white as she'd recommended. Peter Fairchild's stained glass fanlight sparkled over the door. Since her last visit, someone had come to prune the trees and the old oaks looked renewed. The flower beds were planted with bright-faced pansies and a recently installed sprinkler system soaked the newly sodded lawn. Everything was updated, but the spirit of the original house was still intact.

James must have been watching for her because he opened the front door before she had a chance to knock and ushered her in proudly.

"I'm impressed," she said as she looked around the foyer. Light from the new chandelier played over the oak floors and banister. An old-fashioned church pew was tucked against the stairwell wall and a tall pine hall tree faced it from the other side.

In the living room, the big fireplace was still the focal point. James had eschewed authentic Victorian furnishings for his house because he found them plodding and oppressive. Instead, he'd opted for a warm mixture of Shaker-style reproductions and American country antiques. Colly recognized many of the pieces as items she'd helped him choose and resisted the strong temptation to arrange them a bit differently.

"Do you approve of the way the decorator used everything?" he asked. "I wasn't too sure when she suggested a red, white and blue color scheme, but I think it works, don't you?"

She assured him that it did. The colors were muted hues and created a cheerful but masculine setting. Unlike her own house, James's contained a paucity of knickknacks and its uncluttered look appealed even to Colly's collector's eye. "It's a big change from the condo."

He looked around at the wing chairs and woven rugs, the old pine display cabinets and book-lined shelves. "It really is. The condo was cold and this place is warm. I don't know why, but I like it. It feels permanent, like a real home. It's no longer just a place where I keep my stuff."

"What are you going to do with your other furniture?"

"I forgot to tell you. I sold the condo furnished. The guy who's buying it is thrilled to get all that leather and glass and chrome. It'll save him hours of shopping."

He took her arm to show her the rest of the house. The upstairs was as tastefully decorated as the downstairs. Four big bedrooms were filled with sunshine and the kind of beckoning comfort that welcomes you at the end of a long day. Because her imagination was so vivid, it was easy for Colly to imagine herself alongside James in the poster bed that dominated the master bedroom.

He'd have his papers and contracts spread all over the quilted counterpane and she'd be thumbing through a collector's journal, impatient for him to stop thinking of business and start thinking of pleasure. She'd touch him and he'd forget all about work. He would turn off the hurricane lamp...or maybe he'd leave it on. The night would be theirs.

The image was so vividly disturbing that Colly had trouble commenting on the rest of the house. They ended up downstairs in the kitchen where Brigit was polishing silverware that clearly needed no polishing. She greeted Colly warmly before going back to her work.

James led Colly out to the white painted sun porch and they waved at J.J. who was running around the backyard with Harley. The pup had grown considerably since Christmas and was as long-legged as J.J. had become.

They settled into wicker chairs and Brigit brought them glasses of iced tea. "I came early to help out," she reminded James. "Not to be waited on."

"There'll be plenty of time for that. I want to talk to you before the others arrive."

"About what?"

"You haven't said much about it for the past few months, but I'm sure you're wondering what I'm planning to do about J.J."

"Yes, I am. But I knew it had to be your decision."

"I've made quite a few transatlantic phone calls to Lenore and we've finally come to an agreement."

Colly's stomach knotted in anticipation and she would have crossed her fingers if they hadn't been in plain sight. "And what is that agreement?"

He reached inside his coat pocket and withdrew a sheaf of folded papers. As he handed them to her she noticed the official-looking seals and stamps. Holding her breath, she quickly scanned their contents.

She looked up and found James watching her intently. "Oh, James. You've got permanent custody. That's wonderful. I'm so happy for you and for J.J."

"It wasn't an easy decision to make. In the end, Lenore helped me choose."

"In what way?"

"She got married in Europe. Her new husband is a location scout for a big movie company and travels all the time. Of course, she wants to travel with him, but that would be pretty hard to do with J.J. starting school and all."

"So she volunteered to give you custody?"

"Oh, no. Nothing that easy. She still wanted to take him to California but he'd have had to stay with housekeepers most of the time."

"You didn't like that idea," she guessed.

"No, I didn't. It took some talking, but Lenore finally agreed to let him stay with me. She'll have him for a month each summer and every other Christmas."

Colly tapped the papers against her knee. "It's all official?"

"She stopped off in Oklahoma City long enough to sign the papers. I met her husband."

"And?"

"He's not a bad guy. He's younger than Lenore, but he seems to love her. They appeared to be happy."

"How did J.J. react to seeing his mother?"

"He didn't. See her, I mean. She explained everything over the phone. She told me it would be best for everyone if they made a clean break, but I think she was afraid she'd change her mind if she saw him. She's really not a bad person."

"Of course she isn't." As a Taurus, James had an incredible tolerance for the shortcomings of others.

"We've talked to J.J. and I think he understands the situation. As you can see, he seems content."

"You did the right thing, James. I've known it all along. You two belong together."

"I'm not kidding myself. I know it'll be hard at times. But I love him and he loves me. Thanks to you, I think I can handle just about anything that comes up. At least for the next ten or fifteen years."

"I knew that all along."

"So we're not just celebrating the completion of the house tonight. We're also celebrating a new beginning."

Colly felt a painful mixture of happiness and sadness, joy and anguish. The future looked bright for James and J.J., but the papers in her hand only served to remind her that in achieving her goal she had insured that she had no place in it. Time was running out and she felt a desperate need to make the most of what was left.

James was confused by Colly's subdued reaction to his news. He'd expected her to be the first to break out the hats and horns. Instead she was staring quietly into her tea.

"Colly?" He moved from his chair to the love seat beside her. He took the glass from her and set it on the table. Using his finger to tip her face up to his, he was surprised when he saw tears welling in her eyes. "What's wrong?"

"Nothing," she lied as she brushed at the traitorous drops. His gaze found hers and her stomach turned over in response.

"A woman like you doesn't cry over nothing," he chided.

"I'm just so happy for you, that's all. When I first met you, your life was a mess by your own admission. Now, you have a beautiful home, a thriving business, and the security of knowing no one can ever take J.J. away from you. I'm happy because in a few short months you've gotten everything you've ever wanted."

"No, not quite everything," he said as he stroked her cheek and looked intently into her dark green eyes. He hadn't gotten everything he wanted. He leaned toward her and her body responded in kind, drawing him like an unstoppable force.

Colly's whole mixed-up being waited for the kiss. She wouldn't make light of this one, she wouldn't tease or playfully dodge his advances as she'd done for weeks. She wanted this kiss. Needed it. She was starved for his touch and when it came she felt like a wilted flower that had just been rained on. Hopeful. Renewed. Alive.

She kissed him with a desperation she hadn't known she possessed and the need rose in her like a fever. It was a good thing it was broad daylight. And better still that they were sitting on a glassed-in porch in full view of everybody. Because if they had any privacy at all, clothes would have to be discarded. Skin would have to touch skin. Urges would have to be satisfied. There would be no stopping.

His hand slipped under her blouse to caress her breasts, and she began to think broad daylight might not be quite inhibiting enough. She felt a fire growing inside her and needed to know what would happen if she allowed it to burn out of control. When he pulled her onto his lap she discovered that his passion was as strong as her own.

How could she let this man out of her life? Better still, how could she keep him in it? She knew nothing about making a man happy. She was in over her head. This was serious, grown-up stuff here. This was the heavy-duty, mindless desire that she'd read about but never experienced.

But was it love?

Before her fevered brain could answer the question, Brigit's cheerful voice called out from the kitchen. "Yoo-hoo! The caterers are here. Would you come and show them where to unload, Mr. Townsend?"

Embarrassed by her wanton behavior, Colly extricated herself from James's embrace. "The master of the house is being summoned," she murmured.

His groan expressed her own disappointment and relief. "That was nice."

She laughed. "Are you kidding? That was fantastic!"

"Yeah, it was. Can we continue this discussion later?"

"Yoo-hoo, Mr. Townsend!" Brigit hollered.

"I'll be right there." He looked at Colly. "Later?"

"Later," she agreed. The distraction of the party would give her time to think about what had almost happened. She hadn't known until James kissed her just now, how much she wanted him. She wanted everything he had to offer and with a man like James, that would be a lot. So what if she didn't have much experience.

He could teach her everything she needed to know.

Chapter Nine

Midway through the evening Brigit brought J.J. into the living room to say good-night to the guests. Colly knelt to give him a kiss and he explained that he was going home with the housekeeper to spend the night. Brigit's church was sponsoring a special children's program Sunday morning and he had to get up early to attend.

After saying good-night to his son, James mingled with his guests, answering their questions about the renovations with a knowledge and enthusiasm he never expected to possess. Six months ago he gave very little thought to his dwelling or its contents. Home was simply a place to return to when he had no place else to go. Now here he was discussing the pros and cons of oil-based paint like a true homeowner.

The transformation wasn't as miraculous as it seemed. Colly had awakened him to a whole world of possibilities. If everything went as he hoped, they could explore those possibilities tonight. He eased out of a conversation with one of his employees and sidled over to the buffet table where she was arranging sandwiches on a plate.

"Are you still planning to stay after the others leave?"

"That could be arranged. What do you have in mind?"

He didn't dare tell the truth. "I thought you might help me find a good place to display the decoy." She'd given him an antique wooden duck as a housewarming gift.

"Anything for the duck." She saw through the pretense and smiled, and her heart beat faster at the thought of being with James in the full sense of the word. She wouldn't deny her feelings tonight. If she couldn't express them verbally, she'd try to express them physically.

He gave her a quick kiss and squeeze. Glancing impatiently at his watch he whispered, "How long do these housewarming things last, anyway?"

It was two hours before the last of the guests departed. Colly helped James straighten up the kitchen and wrap and store the leftover party food. Finally there was nothing else to do but acknowledge the fact that they were all alone in the house.

They went out to the sun porch, which at night was a dark quiet place, full of shadows and the scent of spring. Moonlight streamed through the open windows along with the nocturnal sounds of nature. Crickets chirped in the grass, night birds twittered in the trees. Out in the big oak, a gentle breeze rustled the new leaves and stirred J.J.'s swing to creaky movement.

Taking her hand in his, James led Colly to the wicker settee and sat down beside her. "Thanks for everything."

She intentionally misconstrued his meaning. "All I did was stack a few sandwiches and refill the punch bowl."

"No, Colly. You've done far more than that and you know it. Thank you for helping me be what I could be. You taught me to value what I had and to view each day as a gift. I've learned a lot from you, teacher, but the most important thing is that family comes first."

"I teach best by example."

"So do I."

His lips covered hers and Colly felt more cherished than she ever had. After long delicious moments, he drew away.

The kiss was to give him the courage to say what he was determined to say. For weeks, James had wanted to share his feelings with Colly, to tell her how much she'd come to mean to him. He loved her but he knew love wasn't enough to overcome the problems they faced. So, he'd put his priorities in order and worked hard to resolve those problems. Now, at last, he could offer her a life with a minimum of complications.

The house, which deep down he knew he'd bought for her, was complete. The custody question was settled and he felt confident in his parenting role. His business was running smoother than it ever had now that he delegated some of the work load to others. He'd made peace with his mother and no longer felt guilt or regret about that relationship.

He'd gotten rid of the static in his life. He had systematically eliminated as much tension and pressure as possible. He couldn't guarantee he'd never again succumb to the stress of living in a confusing world, but he was no longer addicted to it. He finally had something to offer Colly.

A love he'd never felt for another woman and the time to make their dreams come true.

"I love you, Colly," he told her. "I've wanted to tell you for a long time now, but the timing wasn't right."

His words caught her off guard. "You don't have to tell me you love me," she whispered.

"There's no 'have to' about it. I need to tell you."

She sat quietly, her emotions in conflict. Was this a prerequisite for lovemaking? Luz and other friends claimed men often said such things because they thought women wanted to hear them.

He hadn't yet sensed her uncertainty and smiled against her cheek. "I'm glad you decided to stay with me tonight. It's time we talked and worked out our plans."

She wasn't sure if it had been a conscious decision or whether she had simply allowed it to happen. Either way, there was no turning back now.

"I want this night to be special for you, Colly."

"It will be." It would be a night she would remember always. She wrapped her arms around his neck and brought his lips to hers where they belonged. Didn't he realize that she didn't need declarations of undying devotion? All she needed was James, warm and tender in her arms.

Taking the initiative before her courage could desert her, Colly made quick work of the buttons on his shirt. She reached up to tug it off his shoulders. Giving in to the need building inside her, she trailed her hands down his chest, enjoying the shiver of desire she felt under them. She leaned against him, wrapped her arms around his strong body and squeezed hard.

"I want you so much. I've never felt this way before."

"How do you feel, Colly?"

"Like I won't be able to continue breathing unless I touch you—every bit of you—very soon."

"That can also be arranged." James was intoxicated by her words and by her passionate response. She was warm, soft and willing. Desire so overshadowed his other emotions that he almost forgot to ask her to marry him. When he forced himself to think about it, he realized that it was right that he should propose here, in the house that had been meant for her from the start.

"Will you marry me, Colly?" He feathered kisses over and around her mouth, then gazed into her wide, green eyes, waiting for her answer.

She slumped against him. "You needn't propose to me, James. I'm more than willing to do anything we can think of doing together."

He leaned back to look at her. Moonlight shimmered in her hair and glittered in her eyes. "What are you talking about?"

"I'm inexperienced, James, but I don't need declarations. I'm willing."

"Willing to what?"

"To... you know." Her embarrassment was acute. Why were they discussing this?

"I think we're talking about two different things here." His tone was impatient. "I'm talking about us being a family, about spending the rest of our lives together, and you're talking about sex."

"I was thinking about tonight," she clarified. "Obviously, you're thinking about forever." Everything was happening too fast. She'd known when she agreed to stay after the party that he had something in mind. She hadn't expected a marriage proposal.

"Tonight's not enough for me, Colly." He shrugged into his shirt and silently cursed himself as he buttoned it. He'd done exactly what he'd sworn not to do—he was rushing her, asking for too much. He couldn't help it.

"I want more than a night of lovemaking. I want a lifetime. I want to marry you."

"I'm not ready for that, James," she said quietly.

"When do you think you might be ready?"

She sighed again. Either she wasn't speaking plainly or he wasn't listening. She wished words hadn't gotten in the way of actions. "I don't know."

"I'm a patient man. I can wait."

She knew he would. The Taurus patience was legendary. "That wouldn't be fair to you."

His tone was maddeningly calm, considering the turn of the conversation. "I'll be the judge of that. How long do you need, Colly? How long will it take you to acknowledge your feelings? A month? A year?"

"It's not a question of time. I can't marry you."

"Why not?"

"Because you don't really love me."

He shook his head in confusion. "Didn't I just say I loved you?"

"You said it, but you don't really mean it. I've thought about it a lot and I've decided that what you really feel for me is gratitude."

"Oh? You've decided, huh?" He'd gone from patient to impatient very quickly.

"You're thankful for all the help I've given you, you said so yourself."

"Well, yes, but that's not all of it."

"How can you be sure?" she questioned pointedly. "How do you know you haven't simply mistaken your feelings of gratitude for love? I've become so tied up in your new life with J.J. that you can't separate your feelings."

James was completely amazed. "So you're saying the reason I daydream about you when I should be working

or sleeping is because I'm appreciative of all you've done
for J.J.?''

"That's the gist of it. You repressed your love for J.J.
a long time. You built a wall between the two of you because you were afraid of loving him too much and losing
him. Then he came to stay with you and I was there when
he helped you tear down the wall. The love overflowed.
It's only natural that some of it spilled over onto me.''

"That's an amazing analysis, but I can't believe an intelligent woman would believe it. Of course you're tied
up in our lives. J.J. and I want to make it a permanent
arrangement.''

Colly looked at him in alarm. "Oh, no! You haven't
said anything to him about this, have you?''

"No. I hoped we might give him the good news together.''

She breathed a sigh of relief. "I'm sorry, James. If I'd
thought for one minute that you had marriage in mind,
I wouldn't have let things get so out of hand.''

"Why do you think I bought this house? I knew you
liked it, that it was close to your parents. In light of this
conversation, I guess it was pretty presumptuous of me,
but I planned all along for the three of us to live here together.''

"I always told you that I wanted us to be friends,'' she
reminded him.

"And we are. But we could be so much more.'' He
took her hands in his. He was not a man who loved easily and her rejection wounded him deeply. "Colly, do you
seriously doubt my love or the physical attraction we
share?''

"I have reasonable doubt, yes,'' she admitted. "I don't
think you're being objective.''

"God, I hope not. Love is the most subjective emotion of all."

"You have love confused with something else," she insisted.

"Some things you've said are true," he allowed. "I had built a wall between myself and my feelings. For years, I filled my life with work so I wouldn't have to confront them. I kept myself almost maniacally busy so I wouldn't have the time or energy to notice how little meaning there was in my life—"

"James."

"Let me finish. At first, I was angry with Lenore for running away and making me face my responsibilities. I'm ashamed to admit it now, but J.J. cramped my style. He got in the way. If I hadn't met you when I did, I might have messed up the best opportunity I've ever had. Until you showed me, I didn't know what my relationship with my own son could be."

"You would have discovered it for yourself, it just might have taken a little longer."

"No, I don't think so. You're responsible for helping me get my priorities straight, Colly. You said what I feel is gratitude. That much is true. Why shouldn't I be grateful? You gave me my son back."

"I didn't do so much."

"Yes, you did. You encouraged me and made me believe in myself. I know you've tried to keep a distance between us, but no matter what you say, you're a part of mine and J.J.'s lives. You never misled me, but all along I've thought we meant something to you, that you cared about us."

"I do care, James."

"But obviously not enough."

His words were bitter and Colly hated herself for hurting him. He made her feel cherished, wanted and needed. But it was for all the wrong reasons. By his own admission, she fit into his life because of J.J. That was not enough to build a future on.

"Try to understand, James," she pleaded.

"I am trying." He understood that she was scared. That she was terrified of making the kind of commitment he needed. "I'm trying to understand because I love you. And whether or not you're willing to admit it, I think you love me, too. I fought my feelings for a long time before taking your advice."

"My advice?"

"Don't you remember? You told me to listen to my heart. I can only hope that someday you'll listen to yours."

"I feel something but I don't know if it is love. It could be respect or admiration or even just serious like, for that matter."

"Love is all those things, Colly. And more." She looked so bereft he tried to lighten the mood with humor. "Are you sure you don't love me? Not even a little bit?" As a measuring device, he held up his thumb and finger, a centimeter of space between them, and smiled half-heartedly. "Not even this much?"

She leaned her head against his chest. "At least that much."

"Good. That's enough for now." It was enough to give him hope, anyway.

"You mean you won't give up on me?"

"Not yet." He looked at her in a way that made her heart swell.

"You really are a wonderful man."

"Well, at least we agree on something."

She laughed, relieved that they still had a chance for the future and that her insecurity and doubts had not brought everything crashing down on her foolish head.

He patted her hand. "I don't agree with everything you've said tonight, but I will concede that we still have a lot to work out. You know, it's funny. But in the past, women have been reluctant to get too involved with me once they learned I had a child. I never expected J.J. to be a problem with you."

She hurried to assure him that such was not the case. "Oh, don't think that. I love J.J. If it hadn't been for him we never would have met." He still looked unsure so she rushed on, "In fact, if I hadn't been trying to get you and J.J. together, I never would have gotten involved with you in the first place."

Too late she realized that her words had come out all wrong. She put her hand to her mouth.

At her pained expression, realization dawned and James began to understand her original motives. "J.J. and I were just another project to you, weren't we?"

"No! I mean, maybe at first. That's how it started."

She looked overwhelmed. And guilty. James knew he should say something to make her feel better, but he felt so awful himself that he couldn't think of any comforting words.

"James, say something." The stony look in his eyes scared her.

He knew he had no right to feel betrayed. Colly had never made him a single promise. He'd assumed and presumed, but apparently he hadn't been listening.

He remained silent and Colly endeavored to explain. "When I talked to you on the phone at first, I thought you were...well, a jerk. One of those self-absorbed yuppie parents who measure out quality time by the teaspoon. But when I met you and talked to you, I knew you could be everything J.J. needed. All you needed was a little help.''

"And you felt qualified to give that help?''

"Yes,'' she said simply.

"You had your own private agenda, didn't you? You took it upon yourself to meddle in our lives, to manipulate things to your satisfaction. That's it, isn't it?''

Meddle. There was that word again, come back to haunt her. "I never thought it was meddling.''

"Or manipulating?''

"No. Why are you so mad at me?'' she demanded. "You just told me how much better your life is now. You said it was because of me.''

"You succeeded in accomplishing everything you set out to do,'' he told her scornfully.

Colly felt inadequate to make him understand. "But you're mad at me.''

"I'm furious.''

"Why?'' she cried. She tried to touch him, but he pulled away. When the bull was wounded, the last thing he wanted was comfort. He wanted refuge and found it in angry words.

"Because you thought you knew better than me what I needed. And because you were right. You made me love you and you thought you could just walk away when the job was done. Did you think you could create a new life for me, all clean and unwrinkled like a shirt from the laundry, and not be a part of it?''

She had no answers. Her guilt was too overwhelming.

"In your own impulsive way, you gave no thought to what would happen to me and J.J. when you waltzed out of our lives. That's why I'm mad. It's also why I'm hurt and confused.''

Colly was stunned by James's emotional verbal outpouring. He was right. Of course. Her mother had warned her. Luz had warned her. She hadn't listened. "I can't argue with you. All I can say is, I'm sorry."

"That makes me feel a lot better, Colly."

"I told you I wasn't ready for the responsibilities of love."

"And I can't argue with that. You told me quite often, in fact. In my warped male way, I guess I thought I could help you overcome your insecurities."

"I may in time. Can you forgive me?"

"I may in time." He grasped her arms and made her look into his eyes. "You told me I'd built a wall between me and J.J. Well, it was nothing compared to the fortress you've built around yourself."

"I don't trust myself, James. You and J.J. are solid now, you don't need my uncertainties."

"We need you," he said quietly.

"I'm afraid."

"If I can master my fears, you can master yours."

"I don't know." Sad but vehement, she shook her head. "There's nothing left to say. I'd better go."

"Yes, go," he whispered, his lips inches from hers. "But before you leave here's a little something to take with you. Maybe it'll remind you what you're throwing away."

His mouth captured hers in a fierce caress. He wielded so much power over her senses that Colly could do little more than melt against him.

All too soon, he lifted his head and his breath came fast and ragged. "You do love me," he told her huskily. "I feel it every time I kiss you."

Tears stung her eyes and she willed them not to fall.

He set her gently away from him. "You're young and inexperienced but sooner or later you'll understand what went wrong here. I know it's unreasonable, but it hurts me to think that you were more interested in J.J. than you were in me."

"Only at first—"

"You used our friendship to bring me and my son together. No matter how mad that makes me, I can't hold it against you because your intentions were honorable. I don't approve of your methods, but I still love you. And Colly, it's not me who has gratitude and love mixed up— it's you."

"Earlier you said I could have some time. Are you still agreeable to that?" she asked hopefully.

"I'm agreeable. Take all the time you need, but don't take too long. Even a patient man gets tired of waiting."

Colly managed to hold back the flood of tears until she reached the security of her own home. She'd never been more confused in her life.

She'd achieved the goal she'd set for herself. James had permanent custody of J.J. and they were finally a stable family unit. It was time for her to bow out of their lives. Time to move on to other things.

The problem was, there was nothing as important to her as James and J.J.

The next morning Colly got up red-eyed and depressed. She moped over her morning cup of tea and read the Sunday paper with little interest. She didn't know what she was going to do with herself all day until she read her horoscope.

"Although it is the nature of Aquarius to hide their innermost feelings, today will be different. Talk to a friend and share your problems. You'll be surprised how much better you'll feel."

She called Luz and invited her out to dinner. As it turned out, she didn't have to share a thing. Luz nailed her with questions the moment she arrived.

After Colly had explained what had happened the night before, Luz clucked her tongue. "Girl, how can a woman with your brains be so dumb?"

"It takes lots of practice," she said wryly.

"You're just going to give him up?"

"I have to."

"Why?"

"I'm not ready for the kind of commitment James wants. Everything is going so well in his life, he doesn't need me and my doubts to mess it up."

Luz guffawed. "That's ridiculous, girl, and you know it."

"Luz, you're my friend. I could use your support right now. If this is the kind of help I can expect from you, I don't want it. I'll just stay here and cook my own dinner."

"I'm not about to leave you alone to commit culinary suicide. Besides, I passed up a better offer to come over here and help you nurse your broken heart. You're not going to get rid of me that easy."

"Liar," Colly teased with a grin. "I know Barry's invited to his friend's bachelor party tonight."

"Don't remind me, girl. I have these horrible visions of some beautiful, half-clothed creature jumping out of a cake and into his arms."

"They don't still do that, do they?"

"I don't know and I don't want to think about it. You're incredibly unkind to bring it up."

"I didn't," Colly reminded her. "Are you really worried that Barry would take off with some naked nymph?"

Luz considered that. "Yes and no. I trust him but I don't trust a woman who would jump out of a cake for money."

"I see your point."

"And I see yours. You're trying to make me miserable, thereby changing the subject. It won't work, you know. I intend to talk some sense into you before the day is over. But let's do it at the Olive Garden."

"Italian food? I thought you were on a diet."

"I am, I'll just have salad."

No one could go to the Olive Garden Restaurant and just eat salad. They ended up devouring a basket of buttery bread sticks and big plates of fettuccine Alfredo. As soon as the waiter cleared the table, Luz began her assault all over again.

"So, James didn't appreciate being manipulated into something that would have happened anyway?"

Colly defended her actions. "It might have taken him years to seek permanent custody of J.J. on his own."

"But you know he would have done it eventually. The man has a lot of heart."

"Yes," she agreed.

"I'm surprised he wasn't the one to break it off when he figured out how you'd tricked him. Wasn't he angry?"

"In his own words, he was furious. But I think he was more hurt than anything."

"That proves it." Luz nodded for the waiter to bring the dessert tray to the table. "He loves you."

"That's what he said."

"Otherwise, he would have kicked you out of his house." Luz chose a thick slice of chocolate mint pie and tempted Colly into having half of it.

She sighed. "I wouldn't have blamed him if he had."

"And you love him, too, you're just too afraid to admit it."

"That's not what scares me."

"So what are you afraid of?"

"In a word, love." Even as she said it, Colly realized it was true.

"Girl," Luz admonished. "It scares you because you've never really been in love before. You've been infatuated a time or two, but you've always stayed in shallow water. This time you fell in too deep and you don't know how to swim."

"Nice analogy, Luz. Did you hear it on Oprah?"

"Make fun if you want, but it's true."

"Actually I do know how to swim. You taught me." Luz had been incredulous that Colly could have grown up in a commune and not learned to swim. But she'd always been afraid of water and her parents had never forced her to face her fear. Luz had dragged her immediately to the pool.

"You did fine as long as you knew your feet touched the bottom of the pool." Luz grinned broadly. "Remember the day you jumped off the diving board?"

Colly shivered. "I panicked."

"You fought the lifeguard and nearly drowned him when he tried to rescue you." Luz shrugged. "It's the same thing all over again. Only this time, rather than trusting James to rescue you, you've decided to drown yourself."

Colly made a face. "Now who's being dumb?"

Luz let the remark pass and concentrated on her share of the pie. After a few minutes, Colly asked her, "How do you know that you won't wake up some morning and wish you hadn't married Barry?"

Luz thought about it for a moment, then smiled dreamily. "Because he makes my knees weak."

Colly chuckled. "That's it? You're promising to love and cherish a man forever because he turns your knees to jelly?"

"Is there any other reason?"

"I'm serious."

"It's hard to explain, but I'll try. Just sitting here thinking about spending the rest of my life with Barry makes me happy. He doesn't even have to be present to give me goose bumps in places I never knew I could get goose bumps." Luz sighed. "Does that make sense?"

Colly remembered the kisses she'd shared with James and her heart fluttered wildly in her chest. "Yes, it does."

"See, you're in love! The question is, what are you going to do about it?"

"Nothing."

"Why not?"

"Because I can't be sure it will last."

"Who can, girl? Love's nothing but a crapshoot."

"That's romantic," Colly said with a frown.

"But it's true. You just go with your heart."

"That's what my mother said."

"She's a smart lady. We're both smart ladies. Listen to us, girl."

"Let's go home."

"Come on, Colly—"

"If you're my friend you'll take me home and never bring this subject up again."

Luz crossed her fingers behind her back. "Okay, girl, if that's the way you want it. You know you can always count on me."

Chapter Ten

Weeks passed and Colly made no move to patch things up with James, even though she knew it would be up to her to do so. He was obviously avoiding her. Brigit started dropping J.J. off at school in the morning and picking him up in the afternoon. With only a casual explanation of "having a little extra time on her hands," she took James's place at school, volunteering a few hours each week. James stopped coming to Shady Dell altogether, but Colly didn't have the heart to make an issue of it.

By the beginning of May, Colly was still just going through the motions of living, full of unresolved conflict about her parting with James. She tried not to let her inner turmoil affect her teaching and it was a testament to her acting ability that none of the children seemed to notice anything amiss. But her carefree act was just that—an act.

She felt none of her usual enthusiasm as she took the April bunnies and lambs from the bulletin board and replaced them with May baskets full of construction paper flowers the children had made. Luz was the only one who knew what Colly was suffering, but Colly stubbornly refused to discuss the subject, even with her best friend.

The end of the spring session was near and she busied herself planning the children's graduation ceremony and the reception for parents that always followed.

Hungry as she was to know how James was faring, Colly listened carefully whenever J.J. talked about his father. Given the time they spent together each day, she was kept fairly well informed. When James's birthday came around, she helped J.J. make him a card. She wanted to send one of her own, but wasn't sure how he would interpret the gesture. She settled for sending her birthday wishes via J.J. who explained that he and his father were celebrating at the pizza parlor. She wasn't invited and she tried not to care.

Although she missed him terribly, she didn't really mind that James had taken matters into his own hands and severed his ties with her and Shady Dell. Seeing him as frequently as she had before would have been too painful. Trying to wean herself away from J.J. was difficult enough.

He'd often asked her why she didn't come to see him at home any more and she'd made up feeble excuses each time. But in the end, he seemed happy to see her at school and greeted her each morning with a big hug. His daily presence was a constant reminder of what she had given up. Lately, she'd worried that she'd made a terrible mistake that night after the party, but was afraid to compound it with another.

One warm May afternoon Colly stepped out of her office where she'd been going over the summer enrollment forms. The children had been listening to Luz tell a story with hand puppets and were breaking into small groups for independent play. She stopped J.J. on his way to the block area.

"J.J., did you forget to bring your blue paper today?"

"I'm not comin' back to school after I . . . graduate," he said, proudly manipulating the big word around his small tongue. "Me and my dad are gonna be too busy."

Colly had known J.J. would walk out of her life one day, but she wasn't prepared for the awful reality. "What will you be doing?" she asked in a friendly but not too inquisitive tone.

"Takin' bacations," J.J. informed her.

"That sounds like fun." James and J.J. would be spending the long summer days together, doing things that did not include her.

"Will you be away for the whole summer?"

"Nah." J.J. took a stack of blocks from the shelf and sat down on the floor to construct a tower. "Dad says we can't go too far, 'cause he has to check in with his office. So we're gonna see some of the state parks."

"That'll be exciting. There are lots of things to do there."

"I know that. We're gonna go fishin' and swimmin' and stuff. We bought a little house on wheels and it has a tiny bathroom with a real toilet that flushes." His eyes twinkled. "Dad says I can only flush it when it's absolutely ness . . . a . . . nessasary."

When J.J. concentrated, as he was doing now, he looked very much like James. His eyes and hair were a different color, but his determined chin was a replica of his father's. How she would miss him. Both of them.

"I like flushin'," he added as if she might not be aware of that particular character flaw in children.

"I know, but it wastes water." Her voice sounded as shaky as she felt.

"That's what Dad says."

"Your father's a smart man, you should always listen to him." Her eyes burned with weariness from her sleepless nights.

"I always do. He's takin' me to California before kindergarten starts."

"Oh?"

"I'm gonna see my mama. She's living in a big city with a new husband."

Colly had often wondered about J.J.'s reaction to his mother's defection. Apparently, he didn't view it that way because he went on in an animated voice, "I'm going to live with Dad most of the time and visit Mama. I used to live with Mama most of the time and visit Dad. I think I like livin' with Dad the best."

"Why is that, J.J.?" she asked gently.

"Me and Dad have fun together. He teaches me stuff. He's not as busy as he used to be," he explained. "I like my room and the backyard and having Harley. Dad lets Harley sleep on my bed," he said in a confidential tone. "Mama would never do that 'cause she don't like dogs."

"I know you and your dad are going to have a very happy life."

"And you too, Colly," he said with a smile.

"Me, too."

He finished his tower and looked up at her. "I don't see why you can't come when we go campin'."

Colly took a deep, calming breath. "There are other boys and girls who need me here this summer."

"Miss Luz could take care of 'em."

She couldn't make him understand a situation that she didn't understand herself. "There are so many children that it takes more than one person."

He looked around at his classmates, all involved in engaging activities. "Yeah, I see what you mean."

Colly forced a note of gaiety into her tone that she didn't feel. "Have you been practicing your poem for the graduation ceremony? It's next week."

"Me and Dad are workin' on it. He says I'm the smartest boy he ever knew."

The change in J.J. was nothing short of miraculous. At the beginning of the school year, he'd been shy and withdrawn. Now he was preparing to address a roomful of grown-ups, reading a poem she'd helped him compose. She felt such an overwhelming need to touch him that she ruffled his curls and knelt to whisper in his ear. "Don't tell anyone, but so do I."

J.J.'s newfound pride in himself was partly her doing and no one could take that away from her. She motioned for Luz to take over the class while she escaped to her office for a few moments to regain her composure.

The little graduation ceremony was a week away. She only had to endure a few more days and see James one last time. Then she would never have to suffer the pain of seeing either of them again. But the knowledge that this chapter of her life was coming to a close did not make her feel any better. It made her want to cry.

She wouldn't. She was strong. She could face anything that came her way and handle it with dignity. That's what she was determined to do.

Every child at Shady Dell was encouraged to take part in the graduation ceremony that would mark the end of their preschool career. Memorizing poems and the words to songs, they took the occasion as seriously as any matriculating college senior. They rehearsed for days before the event with the musically inclined Luz leading the pint-size chorus in a medley of tunes.

Colly fitted each child in a miniature white gown and mortar board. They got a bit distracted with the gold tassels, but they finally perfected the technique of flipping them to the opposite sides of their caps when they received their little diplomas.

The big night finally arrived and the main room at Shady Dell was filled with rows of folding chairs for proud parents. A miniature podium was set up in front, complete with sound system. Colly knew from previous years that a microphone was essential. Stage fright prevented some students from speaking above a whisper.

Colly decided to wear the Victorian dress James had given her for Christmas. Since this might be the last time she saw him, she wanted him to know how much his gift had meant to her. She watched for him as she greeted parents, but she had to get busy behind the scenes before he arrived.

Under Luz's direction, the little chorus sang their songs flawlessly as the blinking eyes of video cameras recorded the moment for posterity. The children who were to recite poems stepped up to the mike one at a time. Some stumbled over their lines, some mumbled, and some proved they were orators in the making. J.J. was one of those.

As she busied herself hustling children into their places, Colly noticed James standing in the back of the room. She didn't have time to think about him, because it was soon time to pass out the diplomas.

She stepped forward and directed her comments to the gathered parents. "It's been a great year and I'd like to thank all of you for so generously sharing your time and talents with us. Some of your children will be coming back for the summer and we have a lot of fun things planned, so those parents aren't off the hook quite yet."

Colly waited for the laughter to die down before continuing. "In a few minutes your children will come forward to receive recognition for completing a big step in their educational career. It's been said that in the relative scheme of things, a child learns more in nursery school than he or she learns in college. I'm inclined to agree.

"This year your children have developed social skills that will see them through life. They've learned autonomy, independence and creative problem-solving. Never again will their curiosity and drive to learn be as great as it was in the preschool years and I assure you we've taken advantage of that. Together, we've explored our world and discovered ourselves.

"It happens every year, I set out to teach them and they end up teaching me. Thank you for entrusting your children to me and for giving me a chance to know them."

Everyone applauded and Colly waited for the room to get quiet. She always felt emotional at this moment, but was even more so tonight because of James and J.J. Hoping for a steady voice she quipped, "That's the good news. Now for the bad. Due to a printer's error, the children's diplomas are not ready for this evening. I promise to mail them next week, but in the meantime, we've made up some mock diplomas for the ceremony because everyone rehearsed so well.

"I apologize for the delay and want to emphasize that it's not the piece of paper that's important. The real accomplishment is what we've all learned from each other."

Colly stepped over to the tray of ribbon-tied paper rolls and the mother acting as pianist struck the opening chords of "Pomp and Circumstance." It was a somber piece but the children loved it. They marched out of the adjacent room where Luz had corralled them and their small faces were so serious that Colly had to smile. This was always a happy sad moment for her.

When it was J.J.'s turn to accept his scroll, he grinned and gave her a thumbs-up sign. She smiled, her heart feeling like a stone in her chest. She glanced at the back of the room and her gaze unerringly found James. He was sitting next to Brigit, holding a video camera in his hand.

She hadn't forgotten a single detail of his handsome face or the mesmerizing quality of those big brown eyes. He smiled and her pulses raced. Her knees felt as weak as Luz had said a woman in love's knees should feel. She'd been miserable for the last month, going through the motions of living, feeling nothing but sadness. Her life had felt like winter, cold and gray and barren.

Then James smiled at her and it was summer again. He filled her up with sunshine and warmth. How could she let this man out of her life? She couldn't.

Not when she loved him so much. Seeing him again made her realize that she had nothing to fear. James would never hurt her as she'd hurt him. The love they shared would give them the courage to face whatever uncertainties life had in store for them. She only hoped it wasn't too late.

James watched her intently, taking in her soft flowing curls and wide green eyes. Along with their fake diplomas, she gave each of her students a loving smile and hug. She wore the dress he'd given her, the "bride" dress as J.J. had called it. But Colly wasn't his bride. He felt an overwhelming sadness that he'd let her go. He cursed the pride that had kept him silent all these weeks. He never should have listened to her silly excuses or half-baked psychological digressions. He should have reasoned with her.

But he'd been hurt. Far too hurt for reason. Now that he'd had time to think things over he knew he had to do something, anything, to win her back. Walking out of here tonight with J.J. could be the end of the bright future he'd envisioned for them.

If he let it.

Their gazes met and they stared at each other for a moment. The last child took her diploma and hurried to her seat. Colly stepped up to the mike. Slowly James lifted the camera to his eye and pushed the record button.

Colly was so flustered about his filming her that she momentarily forgot what she was going to say. Luz had to step up beside her and invite everyone to stay for punch and cookies. Colly just stood there, staring at James.

"Get a grip, girl," Luz whispered to Colly when the crowd broke up. "We have at least an hour of mixing and mingling ahead of us and I can't do it alone."

"He's here."

"You knew he would be."

"He keeps watching me."

Luz grinned. "You've been doing a fair amount of ogling yourself."

"Yes, but I didn't know it would be this hard, that he would affect me like this."

Smiling and talking to parents, they made their way over to the refreshment table to help the volunteer parents serve. Luz pointed the punch ladle at Colly. "And just how does he affect you?"

"Usually when I see an old boyfriend, I'm relieved that things never went too far between us. But when I look at James, all I can think of is what might have been."

"Ooh, girl, that sounds serious. I knew Mr. Dream Boat was the one."

Colly grinned. "The one for what?"

"You know which one. You're crazy in love with him and you want to marry him. Or maybe you just *want* him."

Embarrassed, Colly poked her friend in the ribs. "Someone will hear you."

"I hope you will," Luz said with mock disgust. "Where do you want him? In bed?"

Colly felt her cheeks heat up. "Yes," she whispered.

"Waking up with his arms around you every morning would be heavenly, huh?"

Colly nodded. "Of course, but—"

"Sharing breakfast with him would be a great way to start the day?"

Colly nodded again, her mind filled with visions of the two of them puttering around the kitchen in various stages of undress.

"And wouldn't it be nice and comfortable to know that you could stop anytime during the day and call him? Just to hear his voice?" When Colly nodded, Luz went on, "Wouldn't it be wonderful to have his head on the pillow next to yours, should you suddenly think of something you'd forgotten to tell him?"

Colly nodded and smiled at the parents and children as she passed out punch cups. Luz had carefully kept her voice low, but Colly was horrified to think someone might overhear.

"Let's talk about this later, shall we?" she said out of the corner of her mouth to Luz. She turned to exchange pleasantries with one of the mothers in the line. She could make Luz stop talking about it, but she couldn't make herself stop thinking about it.

James was the most lovable man she'd ever met and he affected her like no other ever had. She knew in her heart that an affair never would have been enough for her, either. It might relieve some of her frustration, but it would do nothing for her emotional state. She'd still be in love with him.

"Marry him, dammit." Even when Luz's tone was hushed her words carried impact. "Trust him. And yourself."

Colly grinned. "I think maybe I do."

Luz clapped her shoulder. "Now you're talking. But save that sentiment for the wedding."

Colly's next punch customers were James, Brigit and J.J. They chatted briefly and inconsequentially for a moment before moving on. Brigit gave her a special smile and James gave her a lingering look.

Somehow Colly got through the rest of the evening. When she'd finally worked up the courage to speak to James in private, she couldn't find him.

"Luz, have you seen James?"

"You mean you haven't said anything to him yet?"

"Not yet," she confirmed.

"Great! They just left."

"He didn't even say goodbye."

"After what you've put him through, I can hardly blame him."

Colly felt a knot of panic in her stomach. She'd decided to tell him she'd changed her mind and now he was gone. "Maybe fate is trying to tell me something."

"Fate, shmate," Luz scoffed. "What about your horoscope for today?"

"What about it?"

"You don't remember?"

"I remember." Her astrological message had been full of portent. She'd tried to forget it all evening, but there was no escaping the truth it contained.

"You have an opportunity to constructively rectify a development that hasn't lived up to your expectations. It can be transformed into everything you want it to be, but you'll have to do the transforming. Pay attention and don't miss your opportunity."

"What do I do now?"

Luz sighed. "That's simple, girl. Go get him. I'll lock up for you."

It wasn't until she got into her car that Colly began to worry again. If James was still interested in her, wouldn't he have said something? What if he'd changed his mind?

No, she knew better than that. She believed in him and she believed in herself. It wouldn't be easy, but if they loved each other enough, they could make it work.

After a few blocks, she decided she couldn't just show up at his house without phoning first. She drove home to place the call. Brigit answered the phone.

"Mr. Townsend came home and went straight to the newspaper. He read something and asked me if I'd stay with J.J. while he went for a drive. He didn't say where he was going, but he did say he wouldn't be gone long. Shall I ask him to call you?"

"No, thank you, Brigit. That won't be necessary."

"Colly?"

"Yes?"

"Would you like the number of his car phone?"

"I have it right here."

"When you talk to him, will you give him a message for me? Tell him I was feeling tired and decided to go to bed in the guest room. Tell him there's no need for him to hurry back."

Colly received and understood that message. "Thank you, Brigit, I'll be sure to tell him."

She wasted no time dialing his other number and James answered on the first ring.

"Hello?"

"James?"

There was a slight hesitation. "Yes."

"This is Colly."

"I know."

"I'd like to talk to you."

He sighed. "About what?"

She knew he wasn't going to make this easy. "For one thing, you've been lax about fulfilling your contract lately. You owe me several hours of participation."

That was not what he had expected to hear. "Under the circumstances, I thought it would be better if I stayed away."

"I hope you'll understand that I can't send J.J.'s diploma until you make good on your obligations."

It was a brassy move, but his laugh gave her hope.

"Is this another ultimatum?"

"I believe it is. It worked once before," she said softly. "Will it work tonight?"

"That depends," he said somewhat suggestively. "I'd like to be clear on your motivation this time. It might save trouble later."

She swallowed hard. "Love and marriage."

The line was silent for so long Colly wondered if they'd been disconnected.

There was an undercurrent of excitement in his voice when he finally spoke. "Do you mean that, Colly?"

"With all my heart. Oh, and James, Brigit asked me to give you a message." He laughed again when she relayed it.

"I think I'm being manipulated again," he said.

"Do you mind?"

"Not a bit. I'll see you in a few minutes." The line went dead and Colly recalled their first conversation that had used almost the same words. She marveled at how much they both had changed. She had never expected that phone call would lead to such happiness. She slowly hung up the receiver and a moment later the doorbell rang.

She peered out the peephole before flinging open the door. "James! How did you get here so fast?"

"I was already on your street when you called. I was driving around, trying to come up with some bullet-proof arguments guaranteed to make you realize how much you love me."

Colly threw her arms around his neck and their lips met in a devouring kiss made even more desperate by the lonely nights they'd been apart. Their kiss was as old as time yet as new as their happiness. Their bodies curved together, mouth to mouth, heart to heart. When their breathing became labored, James broke the kiss and trailed his lips to her cheek, to her earlobe.

His voice was husky when he said, "What made you change your mind?" He hesitated, suddenly feeling terribly insecure. "You did change it, didn't you?"

"No," she said as she framed his beloved face with her hands. "I finally accepted what I've known all along."

"For awhile I wasn't sure this was going to work out."

"Good things come to those who wait," she told him. "I still can't believe you were practically in front of the house when I called."

He grinned sheepishly. "As we were leaving the school tonight Luz suggested I stick around and talk to you. When I told her I couldn't, she hinted that I should read your horoscope before I made up my mind."

Colly laughed. "Why, that little conniver."

"She also said if I didn't make you listen to reason, she was personally going to see to it that J.J. flunked pre-school."

Colly hugged him to her. How close she'd come to losing this wonderful man. "I owe her one."

"When I got home, I dug out the paper. I couldn't think of a better opportunity than that of living happily ever after with you. Will you marry me, Colly?"

"Yes, James." She initiated a kiss that made the other one pale in comparison.

When they drew apart, she teased him. "Why, James, I thought you were too practical and logical to believe anything that was written in the stars."

He was so happy to know she would finally be his that he couldn't let her go for a moment. He tugged her tighter into the circle of his arms.

"I'm going to love you and cherish you forever, even if you are a little bit loony," he promised as he reclaimed her lips.

"You've been brushing up on your astrology, haven't you?"

"I figured I needed all the help I could get. I wasn't going to tell you this, but I've learned how to understand both J.J. and myself by reading astrology books."

"Do you understand me, too?"

"No, but I figure I have a lifetime to study the subject."

She laughed. "We're going to be very happy."

"I know," he agreed. "I never would have guessed astrology could point the way to true love."

"There's nothing wrong with looking to the stars." She ran her finger along the firm line of his jaw. "But I must warn you. There are skeptics out there who doubt a way-out Uranian and a stubborn bull can find true happiness together."

"I'm not stubborn," he grumbled stubbornly as he lowered his mouth to hers again. "I'm determined. I always get what I want."

"And I'm so glad," Colly said against his lips.

*　　*　　*　　*　　*

LOVE AND
THE TAURUS MAN

by Wendy Corsi

April showers bring May flowers, and the sentimental Taurus man is just the type to show up on his beloved's doorstep, clutching a bouquet of glorious springtime blossoms. This sweet fellow is often shy about revealing his feelings in words . . . but gestures like this are twice as meaningful! Hiding behind the Taurus man's bashful smile is a romantic heart that's steadfast and true—and once he's given it to a special woman, it's hers forever.

In *ROOKIE DAD, hard-working Taurus man James Townsend is smitten with whimsical Aquarius woman Colly Fairchild. The February flower is the violet and James will appeal to Colly's playful nature by sending her baskets full of the lovely purple blooms. What flowers would the Taurus man give to you?*

The Taurus man understands that the assertive *Aries* woman secretly needs reassurance that he is all hers, body and soul. He'll make her feel positively cherished when he presents her with a bunch of pink and white Sweet Peas, April's fragile flower.

Deep, abiding love is at the core of the relationship between two *Taurus* mates. May's sweet Lily of the Valley represents the link that joins this pair for a lifetime.

The *Gemini* woman is known to fluctuate in her moods and reactions, but a florist's delivery from a "secret admirer" is bound to thrill her. June is the month of roses, and that dozen long stemmed buds could only be from her own dashing Romeo—the Taurus man.

The *Cancer* woman is captivated by beauty—and by her one-and-only, the lovable Taurus man. He'll be sure to brighten her day when he presents her with a hand-picked bunch of Larkspur, July's flower, in a breathtaking blend of blues, pinks and whites.

The *Leo* lady is a pushover for flattery... and the Taurus man knows it. She'll be thoroughly charmed by the sight of her sweetheart clutching an armful of sun-kissed Gladiolus, August's flower.

The ultra-feminine *Virgo* woman will swoon over an old-fashioned nosegay of September's multi-colored Asters—especially when they're personally delivered with a kiss by the debonair Taurus man.

The artistic *Libra* woman will undoubtedly feel inspired when the Taurus man—who shares her good taste—brings her a rare antique vase filled with vibrant Calendulas, the golden flower of October.

November's vividly colored Chrysanthemums are well-suited to the passionate *Scorpio* woman. The Taurus man knows she adores grand romantic gestures, so he'll fill every room in the house with the yellow, purple, orange and red blossoms.

The spontaneous *Sagittarius* woman adores surprises, and the Taurus man won't wait until Christmas to deliver a beautiful bouquet of December's flower, the Narcissus—just to say "I love you."

The traditional, conservative *Capricorn* woman likes nothing better than January's flower, the classic red carnation, and she'll be delighted when the Taurus man invites her out to dinner—and wears one in his buttonhole.

When the Taurus man thoughtfully brings the creative *Pisces* woman a bunch of lovely March Jonquils, she'll find a thousand ways to enjoy them! She'll wear them in her hair, press them between the pages of her favorite love stories, and dry them to make fragrant potpourri.

Each month's flower holds a special meaning that allows lovers to communicate without words. . . .

January's Carnation	*Admiration*
February's Violet	*Faithfulness*
March's Jonquil	*Desire*
April's Sweet Pea	*Departure*
May's Lily of the Valley	*Return of happiness*
June's Rose	*Love*
July's Larkspur	*Lightness, levity*
August's Gladiola	*Strength*
September's Aster	*Variety*
October's Calendula	*Jealousy*
November's Chrysanthemum	*Optimism*
December's Narcissus	*Self-esteem*

COMING NEXT MONTH

#868 DIAMONDS ARE FOREVER—Linda Varner
Written in the Stars
Jeweler Thomas Wright was in the business of making wedding rings for *other* people. But the fascinating Jilly Sullivan soon had the hard-to-catch Gemini putting his designs on her.

#869 FATHER GOOSE—Marie Ferrarella
Police officer Del Santini never thought of becoming a dad—until he delivered Melissa Ryan's baby. Now he couldn't *stop* thinking of the single mom and her child . . . or stop loving them.

#870 THE RIGHT MAN FOR LOVING—Kristina Logan
When former childhood rivals Elizabeth Palmer and Michael Stafford competed for a coveted amusement park advertising account, they had no idea they'd end up in the tunnel of love. . . .

#871 GOODY TWO-SHOES—Vivian Leiber
Nobody could be as innocent as Sabrina Murray, and columnist Drew Carlson set out to prove it. Problem was, he *couldn't*—not unless he acted on the sizzling attraction between them.

#872 HIS FATHER'S HOUSE—Elizabeth Krueger
Five years ago, accused of a crime he didn't commit, Briant McCullough left town—and Samantha Barrister. Now he's back—to clear his reputation and reclaim the only woman he's ever loved. . . .

#873 ALONE AT LAST—Rita Rainville
Social worker Katie Donovan needed time for herself. But sexy contractor Judd Jordan was out to convince her that, while being alone was fine—being *together* was better.

The spirit of motherhood is the spirit of love—and how better to capture that special feeling than in our short story collection...

Curtiss Ann Matlock
Carole Halston
Linda Shaw

Three glorious new stories that embody the very essence of family and romance are contained in this heartfelt tribute to Mother. Share in the joy by joining us and three of your favorite Silhouette authors for this celebration of motherhood and romance.

Available at your favorite retail outlet in May.

SMD92

"GET AWAY FROM IT ALL" SWEEPSTAKES

HERE'S HOW THE SWEEPSTAKES WORKS

NO PURCHASE NECESSARY

To enter each drawing, complete the appropriate Official Entry Form or a 3" by 5" index card by hand-printing your name, address and phone number and the trip destination that the entry is being submitted for (i.e., Caneel Bay, Canyon Ranch or London and the English Countryside) and mailing it to: Get Away From It All Sweepstakes, P.O. Box 1397, Buffalo, New York 14269-1397.

No responsibility is assumed for lost, late or misdirected mail. Entries must be sent separately with first class postage affixed, and be received by: 4/15/92 for the Caneel Bay Vacation Drawing, 5/15/92 for the Canyon Ranch Vacation Drawing and 6/15/92 for the London and the English Countryside Vacation Drawing. Sweepstakes is open to residents of the U.S. (except Puerto Rico) and Canada, 21 years of age or older as of 5/31/92.

For complete rules send a self-addressed, stamped (WA residents need not affix return postage) envelope to: Get Away From It All Sweepstakes, P.O. Box 4892, Blair, NE 68009.

© 1992 HARLEQUIN ENTERPRISES LTD.

SWP-RLS

"GET AWAY FROM IT ALL" SWEEPSTAKES

HERE'S HOW THE SWEEPSTAKES WORKS

NO PURCHASE NECESSARY

To enter each drawing, complete the appropriate Official Entry Form or a 3" by 5" index card by hand-printing your name, address and phone number and the trip destination that the entry is being submitted for (i.e., Caneel Bay, Canyon Ranch or London and the English Countryside) and mailing it to: Get Away From It All Sweepstakes, P.O. Box 1397, Buffalo, New York 14269-1397.

No responsibility is assumed for lost, late or misdirected mail. Entries must be sent separately with first class postage affixed, and be received by: 4/15/92 for the Caneel Bay Vacation Drawing, 5/15/92 for the Canyon Ranch Vacation Drawing and 6/15/92 for the London and the English Countryside Vacation Drawing. Sweepstakes is open to residents of the U.S. (except Puerto Rico) and Canada, 21 years of age or older as of 5/31/92.

For complete rules send a self-addressed, stamped (WA residents need not affix return postage) envelope to: Get Away From It All Sweepstakes, P.O. Box 4892, Blair, NE 68009.

© 1992 HARLEQUIN ENTERPRISES LTD.

SWP-RLS

"GET AWAY FROM IT ALL"

Brand-new Subscribers-Only Sweepstakes

OFFICIAL ENTRY FORM

This entry must be received by: May 15, 1992
This month's winner will be notified by: May 31, 1992
Trip must be taken between: June 30, 1992—June 30, 1993

YES, I want to win the Canyon Ranch vacation for two. I
understand the prize includes round-trip airfare and the two
additional prizes revealed in the BONUS PRIZES insert.

Name _____

Address _____

City _____

State/Prov._____ Zip/Postal Code_____

Daytime phone number _____
                                    (Area Code)

Return entries with invoice in envelope provided. Each book in this shipment has two
entry coupons — and the more coupons you enter, the better your chances of winning!
© 1992 HARLEQUIN ENTERPRISES LTD.   2M-CPN

"GET AWAY FROM IT ALL"

Brand-new Subscribers-Only Sweepstakes

OFFICIAL ENTRY FORM

This entry must be received by: May 15, 1992
This month's winner will be notified by: May 31, 1992
Trip must be taken between: June 30, 1992—June 30, 1993

YES, I want to win the Canyon Ranch vacation for two. I
understand the prize includes round-trip airfare and the two
additional prizes revealed in the BONUS PRIZES insert.

Name _____

Address _____

City _____

State/Prov._____ Zip/Postal Code_____

Daytime phone number _____
                                    (Area Code)

Return entries with invoice in envelope provided. Each book in this shipment has two
entry coupons — and the more coupons you enter, the better your chances of winning!
© 1992 HARLEQUIN ENTERPRISES LTD.   2M-CPN